A FINE AND BITTER SNOW

Also by Dana Stabenow

The Kate Shugak Series

The Liam Campbell Series

The Star Svensdotter Series

A FINE AND BITTER SNOW

Dana Stabenow

St. Martin's Minotaur
New York

www.minotaurbooks.com

Library of Congress Cataloging-in-Publication Data

Stabenow, Dana.
    A fine and bitter snow : a Kate Shugak novel / Dana Stabenow.
      p. cm.
    ISBN 0-312-20548-1
    1. Shugak, Kate (Fictitious character)—Fiction.   2. Women private investigators—Alaska—Fiction.   3. Alaska—Fiction. I. Title.

PS3569.T1249 F56 2002
813'.54—dc21

                  2002022863

First Edition: June 2002

10 9 8 7 6 5 4 3 2 1

**For
Rich Henshaw,
agent extraordinaire**

My thanks to Deidre S. Ganopole, who busted the Chaste by Choice movement when she got married.

An Author's Note

Although the discerning will find some similarities between the imaginary Kanuyaq Copper Mine and the real Kennecott Copper Mine, I have, as usual, taken gross liberties with Alaskan history and geography and—surprise!—they are not one and the same. Which means Mudhole Smith flew tourists into the Kennecott, not the Kanuyaq. My aunt used to work for him, and from the stories I've heard, I don't think he'd have minded a walk-on part in one of my novels.

A Warning

Any resemblance between my imagined Camp Theodore and the real Camp Denali would be wholly the result of the author's overactive imagination. You can't go to the first. You can go to the second, and you ought to.

. . . frost is marrow-cold, and soon
Winds bring a fine and bitter snow.

—Theodore Roethke

A FINE AND BITTER SNOW

1

Mutt leapt to the seat of the snow machine as Kate thumbed the throttle and together they roared twenty-five miles over unplowed road to Niniltna, four miles past the village to the ghost town of Kanuyaq, and up the rutted, icy path to the Step. There, Kate dismounted, postholed through the snow to the door of the Park Service's headquarters, marched down the hall to Dan O'Brian's office, walked in without knocking, sat down without invitation, and said, "Now then. Would you mind repeating to me exactly what you told Ethan Int-Hout this morning?"

"Hi, Kate," Dan said, the startled look fading from his face. "Nice to see you, too."

Hard on Kate's heels, Mutt barked, one syllable, short, sharp, demanding. "All right already, nice to see you, too." He pulled open a drawer, extracted a slice of homemade moose jerky, and tossed it. Mutt caught it on the fly, and lay down, taking up most of the rest of the square feet of Dan's office, looking marginally appeased.

Kate was anything but. "Well?"

"I'm too green for them, Kate."

Kate's spine was very straight and very stiff. "Too green for whom, exactly?"

"The new administration." Dan waved a hand at the map of Alaska on the wall behind him. "They want to drill in ANWR. I'm on record as not thinking it's the best idea the federal government has ever had, and now everyone's mad at me, from City Hall in Kaktovik to the Department of the Interior in Washington, D.C. You should see some of the E-mails I've been getting. Like to melt down the computer." He ran a hand through a thick thatch of stiff red hair that was beginning to recede at his temples, then rubbed both hands over a square face with open blue eyes and a lot of freckles that refused to fade. "I've never wanted to be anything but what I am, a park ranger in Alaska. But hell, I don't know. The secretary won't even listen to her own employees. They want to drill. And they're looking at Iqaluk, too."

"I beg your pardon?" Her voice had gone soft, marred only by the growling sound caused by the scar on her throat. Mutt stopped chewing and pricked up her very tall gray ears and fixed Kate with wide yellow eyes.

He flapped a hand. "Nothing to get worried about, at least not yet."

"I'm always worried about Iqaluk," Kate said.

"I know."

"So you've been fired?"

He made a wry mouth. "Not exactly. Invited to take early retirement is more like it." He sighed, and said again, "I don't know, Kate. At least Clinton and Gore had a clue about the environment, or pretended they did. This guy, Jesus." He thrust his chair back and stood up to wander over to the window to stare at the snow piled up to the top of the frame. "I don't know," he said, turning back. "Maybe it's time. I don't know that I can work with these people for four years, and maybe eight. I've got twenty-three years in. And hell, maybe they're right. Maybe it's time for a change of management. Not to mention point of view, because I sure as shit am out of fashion this year. Maybe I do need to move on, buy myself a little cabin on a couple acres, find me one of your cousins, settle in, settle down."

"Yeah, and maybe I need to shoot myself in the head," Kate said, "but it might kill me, so I guess I won't."

He grinned, although it seemed perfunctory.

"Whom did you talk to? Who asked you to quit?"

"Dean Wellington. The head guy in Anchorage. I'm not the only one. They're making a clean sweep, Kate, right through the ranks."

"Whom are they going to replace you with? 'Pro-development' and 'park ranger' don't exactly go together in the same sentence."

He shrugged. "If it was me, I'd replace me with a kid fresh out of college, inexperienced, malleable, easy to lead."

"Someone who will do what they're told without asking any of those annoying little questions like 'What are the adverse effects of a massive oil spill on a biome?' Without doing things like counting the bear population to see if there should or shouldn't be a hunt that fall?"

The grin had faded, and Dan looked tired and, for the first time since she'd known him, every one of his forty-nine years. "When's the last time you had a vacation?" she asked.

He rubbed his face again. "I was Outside in October." He dropped his hands and looked at her. "Family reunion."

She snorted. "That's not a vacation; that's indentured service. I mean a real vacation, white sand, blue sea, drinks with little paper umbrellas in them, served by somebody in a sarong."

"Gee, I don't know, that'd be about the same time you were there."

"I don't vacation," Kate said, "I hibernate. When?" He

didn't answer. "Do me a favor, Dan. Don't say yes or no to your boss. Take some time off, and let me work an angle or two."

"Why?"

"Oh, for crissake." Kate stood up. Mutt gulped the last of her jerky and bounced to her feet, tail waving slightly. "I'm not going to sit around here and pander to your ego. Get out of town."

A genuine smile broke out this time. "That's good, since pandering to my ego isn't your best thing. I'm not going to get out of town, though, even though I am now officially terrified to say so."

"And why not?"

"I've got a girl."

"So what else is new?"

"No, Kate, I mean really. I've got a girl."

She estimated the wattage of the glow on his face. "Why, Daniel Patrick O'Brian, as I live and breathe. Are you, by any chance, in love?"

He laughed. He might even have blushed. "Argghh, the *L* word—don't scare me like that."

"Are you?"

"I don't know. I don't want to leave her, though."

"Who is she?"

"She's waiting tables at the Roadhouse. She's great, Kate. I've never met anyone like her. She loves the outdoors, she loves the wildlife, she hikes and mountain-bikes, and she's a good cross-country skier. She wants to learn how to climb and maybe take on Big Bump with me next summer. She's gorgeous, too." He paused. "I've got at least twenty years on her. I've been afraid to ask her how old she is. I don't know what she sees in me."

"Yeah," Kate said. "Don't worry. I do."

He grinned, a little sheepish. "I'm heading out to the Roadhouse this afternoon. I'll introduce you. And buy you a drink?"

"Sold. See you there." She stopped to survey him from the door. Reassured by the sparkle in his eyes and the reappearance of the dimples in his cheeks, she turned and left, Mutt at her heels, flourishing her graceful plume of a tail like a pennant of friendship.

His smile lingered after they were gone. He had been feeling besieged, and if he was not mistaken, he had just received a delegation from the relieving force.

Well. If his friends—it appeared he did have some after all—were going to fight for him, he could do no less.

His smile widened. And he knew just who to recruit for the front lines. He stood up and reached for his parka.

On the way back down the mountain, Kate thought of all the things she could have said in answer to Dan's question. That he'd been the chief ranger for the Park for eighteen years, after working his way up the Park Service's food chain fighting alligators in Florida and volcanoes in Hawaii. That Park rats knew him and trusted him as no Alaskan trusted a federal park ranger anywhere else in the state. That moose and bears both brown and black wandered regularly through her yard, and that a herd of caribou migrated regularly over the plateau, and that no one in the Park who knew how to shoot or any of their families and friends had ever gone hungry on Dan O'Brian's watch.

That Dan O'Brian had managed, sometimes single-handedly, to maintain healthy populations of every species of wildlife from the parka squirrel below ground to the bald eagle above, and had managed to do it while maintaining the good opinion of park rats Native and nonnative, sourdough and cheechako, subsistence hunter and big-game hunter, subsistence fisher and sports fisher and commercial fisher alike, and that he had managed to do it without being shot, or hardly ever shot at, was a remarkable achievement. If some wet-behind-the-ears, fresh-out-of-college kid wired through his belly button to the current administration took over, the Park would begin to deteriorate, and the population of the wildlife would only be the beginning. Mac Devlin would roll out his D-9 and start flattening mountains and damming rivers with the debris in his search for new veins of gold. Dick Nickel would start chartering sports fishers by the 737 into the village airstrip. John Letourneau would start bringing in European big-game hunters by the 747, if he didn't already. Dan O'Brian was just a finger in the dike, but he had it stuck in a pretty vital hole.

Besides, if he left, she'd miss him.

She stopped in Niniltna to talk to Auntie Vi, who listened in bright-eyed silence, her head cocked to one side like a bird's. "I'll start calling," she said, and displayed a cell phone with pride. It was lime green and transparent.

Kate recoiled, as if someone had offered her a diamondback rattlesnake. "Uh, great, Auntie. I'm going to talk to Billy now. And I might go to Anchorage."

"You know somebody there?"

"I can get to know them."

Auntie Vi grinned, and the evil in that grin kept Kate warm all the way to the Niniltna Native Association offices. Billy looked up when she walked into his office. "Ah, and here I was just inches from a clean getaway," he said.

Kate was known in the Park and, indeed, across the state of Alaska for many things. One of them wasn't finesse. "You hear about Dan O'Brian?"

"No."

She told him. As a clincher, she added, "Dan says the feds are interested in selling exploration leases in Iqaluk, too, Billy. We need him."

Billy frowned but said nothing.

Kate was incredulous. "Don't tell me you want to let them drill in Iqaluk!"

"It'd mean jobs, Kate."

"None for us! Nobody here knows how to drill for oil!"

"They could be trained. We could get the feds to make it a condition of the leases."

A hot reply trembled on the tip of her tongue. From somewhere, she found the strength to repress it. "Then," she said, with tight control, "you'd better make sure that we've got the ear of the top spokesman for the feds in this Park."

He frowned. "What do you want me to do?"

"Do you want to have to break in a new ranger? Somebody who's going to go around burning out squatters, even if they've been squatting for twenty years? Somebody who doesn't know a moose from a caribou and won't look the other way when somebody shoots one to feed his kids after the season is closed? Somebody who'll let all the fish go up the river because the lobbyist for the sports fishers has a bigger bullhorn and a fatter wallet than the lobbyist for the commercial fisher?" She paused and took a deep breath. "I'll fight against any kind of development in Iqaluk, Billy, barring the logging leases we've already signed, but if you decide you want to go after subsurface mineral development and you get your way, it's better for all of us to deal with Dan, someone who knows us and knows our ways, than some yahoo with a diploma so new, the ink isn't dry on it yet. At least Dan listens to what the elders have to say about the history of salmon runs. The seals are coming back to the Sound today because he did." She paused again. "You know you don't want to have to break in somebody new."

"Well," Billy said, a defensive look on his round moon face. There was only one right answer, and they both knew what it was. "No."

"All right, then. Call everyone you know in Juneau and then start in on D.C. NNA's got a lobbyist, doesn't it?"

"Yes."

"Call him and tell him the Niniltna Native Association, the largest private landowner in the Park, has a good working relationship with the current chief ranger and how you'd hate to see that change. In fact, you'd hate it so much that any new ranger appointed in his place would very likely meet with resentment and possibly even active opposition. You can't vouch for his or her safety. Mention tar and feathers."

Billy laughed. Kate stared at him. The laughter faded. What Kate Shugak lacked in finesse, she more than made up for in force of personality. Besides, Billy was, above all else, a smart politician and he knew what a poll of Park rats would say about Dan O'Brian leaving office. He cleared his throat and reached for the phone.

Kate made a couple of other stops to talk to village elders, and she was satisfied with their responses. Screw with one of us, screw with all of us, and Dan had been a Park rat long enough that he was definitely on the inside looking out. Mutt, riding behind her, nose into the wind, seemed to sense her feelings and took a swipe at Kate's cheek with her tongue, nearly dislodging the bright red knit hat crammed down over Kate's ears.

On the way to the Roadhouse, she had an inspiration, and five miles short of her goal, she took a turnoff that led down to the river, a mile from the road at this point. Spruce trees stood tall and thick next to a narrow track, snow up to the lowest branches, only to fall into deep declines nearer the trunk. It took some doing not to slide into them, and after the second near miss, Mutt decided to get off and walk. Kate slowed the machine to a crawl and thought about the man she was going to see.

John Letourneau lived on the Kanuyaq River, about a mile downstream from Niniltna. Home was an immense lodge built of peeled spruce logs, with the wall facing the river made almost entirely of glass. He had his own septic system, so there were flush toilets. He had his own well, so there was running water. He had his own generator, so there were electric lights.

It slept twenty in single rooms, each with a private bath, in season, which was as large as he allowed his parties to get. In season was from late June, when the kings started hitting fresh water, until mid-October, when the hunting season ended. There was a miniseason around breakup, when the bears woke up and their coats, which had been growing all winter while they were hibernating, were at their best. He was thinking of starting a second miniseason in January, to take advantage of the prolific tendencies of the Kanuyaq caribou herd.

Letourneau Guides, Inc., offered the thrill of the chase and the satisfaction of the kill, a trip into the primal past, where men could get back in touch with their inner hunter, who killed the night's meal with his bare hands—and a .30-06—and bore it home in triumph, to be awarded the best seat next to the fire and the choicest bits of meat. Not to mention best pick of whatever young virgins happened to be handy.

Young virgins, John couldn't provide, although there were occasionally women among his hunters. He couldn't keep them out because he couldn't necessarily tell from a letter who was a man and who was a woman, and as long as their Visa cards went through and their checks didn't bounce, he didn't care. He cut them no slack, however: They had to keep up, and no whining. If it came to that, he'd had a lot more whining from his male clients, not that he was ever going to say that out loud to anyone. Especially the ones who, because they'd outfitted themselves at REI before they came, figured they had the backwoods about whipped.

It was his pleasure, Kate thought perhaps his very great pleasure, to show them, at their expense, that they didn't.

She'd never heard him go so far as to say that he was in

the business of making men from boys. But he did not deny that it sometimes happened. He housed them well, he fed them very well, and he ran their asses off all over the taiga. They came home most nights to a hot shower and a soft bed, and sometimes, if it was that kind of party, a woman in that bed, on the house. He wasn't averse to a little of that kind of entertainment himself. No loud parties, however, no boozing, and everyone behaved themselves and treated their companions like ladies or they were on the next plane out.

Usually, his clients went home with at least one trophy, and the smart ones took the meat, too. When they didn't, he handed it out to elders in the Park, because he was a man who could see the value in getting along with one's neighbors. Next to the Niniltna Native Association, he was probably the village of Niniltna's biggest taxpayer, and he paid up in full and on time.

He'd been around since the sixties. He'd started out fishing in Cordova, learned to fly, and homesteaded on the Kanuyaq. He started advertising salmon fishing parties and guided hunts in *Field & Stream* in 1965—tent camping, it was back then. He'd built the lodge in 1969, for cash, and from that day forward had never run empty.

He lived alone. The chef arrived with the salmon and departed with the last moose rack. So did the maids and the groundskeepers and the gardener and the boatmen. In the winter, he cooked his own meals and made his own bed, and spent the rest of the time trapping for beaver and mink and marten and curing their skins, which he took into Fur Rendezvous in Anchorage every February and sold at auction.

He didn't have much truck with religion. He drank some, mostly hard liquor. He collected his mail regularly at the post office, and spent enough time at Bernie's to keep up on what was going out over the Bush telegraph, and to avoid the label of hermit. He had not the knack of making friends, and so his winters were solitary. Kate had the feeling that dignity and a spotless reputation meant more to John Letourneau than anything as messy as a relationship.

She pulled up by the front of the porch, giving the motor a couple of unnecessary revs to give him warning. He was waiting at the door by the time she got to the top of the steps. "Kate," he said.

"John," she said in return. Mutt gave an attention-getting sneeze behind her, and she turned, to see the big yellow eyes pleading for fun. "Okay if my dog flushes some game?"

"Turn her loose."

"Thanks. Go," Kate said to Mutt, and Mutt was off, winging across the snow like an enormous gray arrow, head down, tail flattened, legs extended so that they looked twice their normal length.

"Be lucky to see a ptarmigan again this year," John commented as he closed the door. "Coffee?"

"Sure."

He got a carafe out of the kitchen, along with a plate of shortbread cookies. Conversation was restricted to "please" and "thank you" until he had finished serving her and had taken a seat across the living room, at a distance that almost but didn't quite necessitate a shout for communication. The interior of the lodge was very masculine, sparingly but luxuriously furnished with sheepskin rugs, brown leather couch and chairs, heads of one of each of every living thing in the Park hanging from the walls. No humans that Kate could see, but then, it was a big place.

It didn't look all that lived in to her, but it fit him. He was a tall man with a lion's mane of white hair, carefully tended and swept back from a broad and deceptively benevolent brow. He looked like he was about to hand down stone tablets. He'd kept his figure, too, broad shoulders over a narrow waist, slim hips and long, lanky legs encased in faded stovepipe jeans, topped with a long-sleeved dark red plaid shirt over a white T-shirt. He had not yet reached an age to stoop, and his step was still swift and sure across the ground. His hands were enormous, dwarfing the large mug cradled in one palm, calloused, chapped, and scarred. His jaw protruded in a very firm chin, his lips were thin, his nose was high-bridged and thinner, and his eyes were dark and piercing. He fixed her with them now. "What can I do for you, Kate?" he said. "I'm guessing this isn't just a social call."

Since she liked social bullshit as little as he did, she greeted this opening with relief. "You'd guess right. It's about Dan O'Brian."

John had always been hard to read, his expression usually remote and unchanging, as if sometimes he wasn't really in the room when you were talking to him.

"What about him?"

"Did you hear they're trying to force him into early retirement?"

"No." He drank coffee. "I hadn't heard that."

"The administration is looking for a change of flavor in their rangers."

He picked up a cookie and examined it. "I can't say I disagree with them."

She smiled. "Come on, John," she said, relaxing back into her chair. "You've got things pretty good right now. You and Demetri are the sole big-game guides licensed to operate in the Park. Between the two of you, you constitute a monopoly. Dan's happy to keep it that way."

He didn't say anything.

Kate plowed on. "Plus, we know him, and he knows us. What if they start making noises about drilling in Iqaluk again?"

"Are they?

"They are in ANWR. I figure if they start punching holes there, they'll look to start punching them other places, too, and Iqaluk is one of the few places in the state that has already supported a profitable oil field."

"Fifty years ago."

"Still. They can make a case that there's more to find. What happens then? I'll tell you. They move in all their equipment, and they either find oil or they don't. If they don't, it's a temporary mess and we hope they don't screw up the migratory herds too much, and don't spill anything into the water that'll screw with the salmon. If they do, it's a permanent mess, requiring long-term remedial work. Who better to deal with either of these scenarios than the guy who's been on the ground for the last twenty years? The guy we know, and who knows us? Who actually listens to us when we tell him we need to cut back on escapement in the Kanuyaq because too many salmon are getting past the dip netters and it's messing with the spawning beds?"

He smiled, a slight expression, one that didn't stick around for long. "You're very eloquent."

Kate dunked a cookie in her coffee. "Thanks."

"What do you want me to do?"

She swallowed. "You host a lot of VIPs here, John, people with power, people with influence. As I recollect, the governor's been here a time or two. So have both senators and our lone representative. Not to mention half the legislature, and past governors going back to territorial days. Call them and ask them to put in a good word for Dan."

He didn't say anything. He was very good at it.

Kate wanted a commitment. "It's in your best interest to do so, John."

"Maybe," he said. "Maybe not."

She looked at him, puzzled. "Why wouldn't it be?" She searched her mind for any Park legends involving a confrontation between the chief ranger and its biggest guiding outfit, and came up zip.

"It's personal," he said, dumbfounding her. He got to

his feet. "That all you wanted? Because I was about to go out when you drove up."

She set down her mug, still half-full, and her cookie, only half-eaten, and got up. "Sure. Thanks for listening. You'll think about it?"

"I'll think about it."

Personal? she thought as she drove away. John Letourneau had something "personal" going on with Dan O'Brian?

She was pretty sure the earth had just shifted beneath her feet.

The Roadhouse, a big rectangular building with metal siding, a metal roof, and a satellite dish hanging off one corner, was packed right up to its exposed rafters, but then, it always was the day after Christmas. People came from all over the Park to show off their presents, drink away the fact that they hadn't received any, and generally recover from an overdose of family.

Dandy Mike was dancing cheek-to-cheek with some sweet young thing, but he winked at Kate as she threaded her way through the crowd. Bobby and Dinah held court in one corner, baby Katya on Bobby's lap, resplendent in a bright pink corduroy kuspuk trimmed with rickrack and wolverine, necessitating a brief deviation from Kate's course. Katya saw Kate coming, and as soon as Kate was within range, she gathered her chubby little legs beneath her and executed a flying leap that landed her on Kate's chest.

"Oof!" Kate almost went down under the onslaught.

"Shugak!" Bobby bellowed. "Good ta see ya. Sit down and have a snort!"

Kate exchanged sloppy kisses with Katya and exchanged a grin with the ethereal blonde who was her mother. "Hey, Dinah."

"Hey, Kate."

An unknown blonde with melting blue eyes and a figure newspaper editors used to call "well nourished" came over, inspecting Kate with a quizzical eye. "What can I bring you?"

"You know Christie Turner, Kate?"

Aha, Kate thought. "We haven't met, but I've heard tell."

Christie cocked an eyebrow. "Oh, really?"

Kate grinned. "I was just up to the Step."

Christie ducked her head and appeared, in the dim light, to blush. A shy smile trembled at the corners of her mouth. "Oh." That was almost textbook, Kate thought, watching, but then Christie rallied to her duty. "Can I get you a drink?"

The Park was like a desert in midwinter—it sucked every drop of moisture out of the body, caused lips to crack, hangnails to sprout, and an unquenchable thirst for anything in liquid form. "Club soda with a wedge of lime would be good. One of the big glasses."

Ben E. King came on the jukebox. "You've got baby duty," Bobby told Kate, and snatched Dinah's hand and rolled his wheelchair out onto the dance floor.

"Da-deee! Da-deee!"

"You'll have to get taller first," Kate told her.

Mandy and Chick were jitterbugging. Old Sam was watching a game on television and doing the play-by-play, since the sound was turned down. "Where's the defense? Where the hell is the defense? Jesus H. Christ on a crutch, just give him the ball why don'tcha and tie a bow on it while you're at it!" The First Nazarene congregation, consisting of three parishioners and one minister, was holding a prayer meeting in one corner. A group of Monopoly players huddled around one table, with no attention to spare for anything but buying property, acquiring houses, and collecting rent, not even for Sally Forrest and Gene Mayo, who were all but having sex on the table next door.

All pretty much business as usual at Bernie's.

"Kaaaay-tuh," Katya said.

"That's me," she told her, and they rubbed noses in an Eskimo kiss.

Katya leaned over in a perilous arc to tug at one of Mutt's ears. "MMMMMMMMMutt," Katya said.

Mutt endured, looking resigned at this assault on her dignity and person.

The song ended and Bobby and Dinah came back to the table. Bobby gave Kate a salacious grin. "How'd you like to keep Katya overnight?"

"Bobby!" Dinah smacked her husband without much sincerity. "Behave."

"Why? That's no fun," he said, and kissed her with a mixture of gusto and conviction that involved a certain amount of manhandling, which appeared to be received with enthusiasm. Sally and Gene had nothing on these two.

"Jesus," Kate said, "get a room," and perched Katya on her hip for the walk to the bar. Bernie, what hair he had left caught in a ponytail, intelligent eyes the same brown as his hair set deeply in a thin face, had a stick of beef jerky and Kate's club soda waiting. Mutt exchanged a lavish lick for the jerky and lay down at Kate's feet, where everyone was very careful not to step on her.

It was crowded that afternoon, full of talk and laughter, loud music and smoke, and the clink of glass, the pop of bottle caps, and the fizzle of soda water. Bernie was constantly in motion, sliding up and down the bar as if on skates, dispensing beer, screwdrivers, red hots, rusty nails, salty dawgs, and, for one foolhardy table, Long Island iced teas all around, after delivery of which, Bernie confiscated everyone's keys and designated Old Sam Dementieff to drive them home in his pickup. Old Sam got out his martyr look, but fortunately they all lived in Niniltna and he accepted his assignment with minimal grumbling. Bernie returned to his post, and Kate, folding straws into weird shapes for Katya, said, "You hear about Dan O'Brian?"

"What about Dan O'Brian?" a deep voice said, and Kate looked around, to find Alaska state trooper Jim Chopin towering over her. He couldn't help towering, of course; he was six foot ten and she was five foot nothing, but she disliked being towered over, and she let it show.

A weaker man might have been intimidated. Jim appropriated a stool and sat down next to her, close enough to brush sleeves. At her earliest opportunity, which was immediately, Mutt reared up, two enormous paws on his thighs, and submitted to a vigorous head scratching, an expression of bliss on her face that Kate considered extreme. Katya said, "Jeeeeeeeem!" and made her usual aerial launch to her next favorite person. The trooper fielded her like a bounce pass and settled her into his lap. "How about a Coke, Bernie? And a Shirley Temple for my girlfriend." To Kate, Jim said, "What's this about Dan O'Brian?"

Kate bristled. "What's it to you?"

Old Sam, sitting on the other side of Jim, looked into the depths of his beer glass and shook his head. Bernie rolled his eyes, only because Kate wasn't looking at him. Jim's face remained inscrutable, although his blue eyes did narrow.

"They're trying to force him into early retirement," she said grudgingly. "The new administration wants to bring in their own people."

"And you thought I wouldn't be interested?" Jim pulled off his ball cap and ran his hand through a thick mat of carefully cut blond hair. "I live here, too, Kate. And work here, and I work pretty well with Dan O'Brian. He's a good man." His smile was meant to be disarming. "Plus, I don't want to have to break in somebody new."

She owed him an apology. She would have walked over hot coals before she offered it. "Do you have a useful suggestion to make, or are you just talking because you love the sound of your own voice so much?"

A brief silence. She refused to drop her eyes, ignoring the heat climbing up the back of her neck. Bernie brought Jim a Coke, took the temperature of the silence lingering over this section of the bar, decided that discretion was the better part of valor, and busied himself with restocking the beer in the cooler.

Jim took a pull of his Coke. "Have you talked to Ruthe or Dina yet?"

She stared at him.

Old Sam thumped the bar. "Damn good idea."

Jim kept a steady gaze fixed on Kate's face.

Kate drained her glass and set it down on the bar with exquisite care. "Good idea," she said, forcing the words out. "I'll take a ride up there, see if they're home." She held out her arms and Katya flung herself into them.

"Why?" Jim said, handing over the baby. "They're right over there."

Kate looked where he was pointing. "Oh." She gave a stiff nod. "Thanks."

The two men, three when Bernie sidled up, watched her very straight back march off. "Woman sure is on the prod," Bernie said.

Old Sam raised his glass of Alaskan Amber draft and regarded it with a thoughtful expression. "Yea-yah," he said. "Been thinking I'd have a word with Ethan Int-Hout."

"About what?" Bernie said.

Old Sam took a long, savoring swallow. "Been thinking I'd tell him to shit or get off the pot."

Jim turned to stare at Old Sam.

Old Sam, well aware of the stare, gazed limpidly at his own reflection in the mirror on the wall at the back of the bar, what he could see through the standing forest of liquor bottles. "Make things easier on everybody all the way around when that broad has a man in her life."

Jim turned on his stool so he could look Old Sam straight in the eye. "You mean she doesn't now?"

Old Sam cast his eyes heavenward. "Some men," he said to Bernie in a withering tone of voice, "some men purely have to be taken by the pecker and led." He shook his head and finished his beer. "How up are you on your Bible studies, Sergeant?"

"Way down," Jim said.

"Read up on Jacob," Old Sam said, and moved to a table with a better view of the game to continue his play-by-play. Michael Jordan was back, and Old Sam was way more interested in that than he was in anybody's love life.

He didn't look much like Cupid, but then, he'd never much cared for Ethan Int-Hout, having been corked by his father a time or ten out on the fishing grounds. In his eighty years on the job, Old Sam had had some earned life experience in the dictum, Like father, like son.

And in Like grandmother, like granddaughter. Ekaterina had never been one to go long without a man, either.

2

Kate felt the exact moment when Jim Chopin stopped watching her walk away, and she breathed easier for it, although she would have died before admitting it. By the time she got to Dina and Ruthe's table, the two women were out dancing on the floor, with whom, Kate couldn't quite tell. The song was "Gimmee Three Steps," and pretty much everyone was out there, but Dina was easy to find because of her cane, and where Dina was, Ruthe would not be far away. Dina wore a black sweatshirt and, with her white hair, looked from behind like a bald eagle. Ruthe, as usual, looked about half her age, and moved like it, too.

As Kate watched, John Letourneau danced into view. So this was where he'd been headed when she knocked on his door. He was dancing with Auntie Edna, who looked like she was having a wonderful time, until John rock-stepped back into Dina, whose cane somehow became tangled in John's legs. John went down and took about three other dancers with him. Christie Turner tripped over the pile and spilled an entire tray of drinks all over John. Everyone got up again, all laughing, except John, who took a step toward

Dina, who held her cane out at arm's length, its rubber tip against John's chest. He batted it away, and then suddenly Ruthe was dancing with him, jitterbugging or bebopping or swing-dancing, or whatever it was called, doing a series of what looked like complicated turns without missing a beat.

John, perforce, went along, as Auntie Edna faded quietly to the table where Auntie Balasha and Auntie Joy were quilting squares and knocking back Irish coffee. As Kate watched, Auntie Vi came in and made a beeline for the table. The four old women put their heads together and spoke earnestly and at length, with much nodding and shaking of heads. Auntie Joy got out a little notebook and a pen and started making a list.

Lynrd Skynrd got the break they were waiting for and the song faded away, punctuated by whistles and applause from the dance floor. And then, oh my, Creedence Clearwater Revival started rolling down the river and Katya let out a "YES!" loud enough to break her auntie's eardrums and made urgent movements toward the dance floor. Dinah and Bobby were already out there, and they welcomed Kate and Katya with whoops of joy. The circle started small and grew, evolving into sort of a conga line that stamped and shimmied and boogied around the bar, between the tables, around Old Sam Dementieff, who was still grimly focused on the game, out the back door and in the front, scooping up people inbound from the parking lot in its wake. Bobby was the heart of the line, the beginning and the ending of it, rocking back and forth to the beat and frugging and shrugging and clamming and jamming and beating the band. The song wasn't long enough for any of them, so it was a good thing when someone put five dollars into the jukebox and the Beach Boys took them all to Kokomo immediately thereafter. Bernie, in response to universal acclaim, turned up the volume, and the roof of the Roadhouse like to come off.

Katya was laughing and clapping her hands. "Clearly," Kate told her, "you are your father's child."

"She got rhythm all right," Jim said at her shoulder, and Kate became aware not only that he had taken part in the conga line but that he was directly behind her, his hands still on her waist. And maybe even a little lower than that.

She was three feet away from him in a single step. He raised an eyebrow. She didn't like the look of it. Neither did she like the look in his eye as it rested upon her, as she couldn't identify it. She knew all his looks and this wasn't one of them.

She looked around for Mutt and discovered to her dismay that Mutt might have taken part in the dance, as well. She was leaning up against Chopper Jim's manly thigh, gazing adoringly up into his face, tail thumping the floor.

Kate, revolted, said, "Mutt!"

Mutt was instantly galvanized and shot to Kate's side. Her expression, to Kate's severe gaze, looked distinctly sheepish. "Stop seducing my dog," she said to Jim without thinking.

The look in his eye didn't change; in fact, it seemed to increase when he smiled, long and slow. "Give me another target."

"Jeeeeem!" Katya said, and held out her arms with another of her blinding smiles.

Kate looked down at her and said, "I'm saving you from yourself right now," and marched back to Bobby and Dinah's table.

"Thanks, Kate," Dinah said, receiving Katya in a four-point landing.

"My pleasure," Kate said.

Bobby fished keys out of his pocket. "Come to dinner?"

"I'd like to," Kate said, looking around. "I wanted to talk to somebody first—hey, where'd Ruthe and Dina go?"

Dinah followed her gaze. "I don't know; I don't see

them. They must have left. Did you see John Letourneau trip over Dina's cane?"

Bobby threw back his head and roared with laughter. "Did I! That Dina."

"She didn't do it on purpose, Bobby," Dinah said.

Bobby roared again. "Given their history, who knows? And who cares anyway? It was fun to watch John Letourneau fall off his high horse. Dignity, always dignity," he said, and started to laugh again. "Ever see *Singing in the Rain*, Kate? Best goddamn movie ever to come out of Hollywood."

"About thirteen times, all at your house," Kate said.

"We can watch it again tonight," he said, waving an expansive arm. "After dinner. So you coming?"

She shook her head. "I've got to talk to Dina and Ruthe."

"Caribou stew," he said.

She wavered, always susceptible to an appeal to her stomach.

"Plus, you need a haircut," Dinah said, giving her a critical look.

Kate shook her head. "I'd like to, but I really have to talk to Dina and Ruthe. It's about Dan. Rain check?"

Dan appeared at the Roadhouse door just as Kate reached it. He saw her, opened his mouth, and then something behind her caught his eye. He smiled, then laughed out loud when Christie, in a floor-mounted launch of which Katya would have approved, landed against his midsection, her legs prewrapped around his waist, and planted a long, intense kiss on his lips. Kate stepped around them. As she passed, Christie raised her head and their eyes met.

Kate looked around to see who the claim was being staked in front of, and she saw Jim Chopin watching. She looked back at Christie, who smiled and buried her head in Dan's shoulder.

Kate shut the door behind her with more force than necessary.

The Roadhouse was twenty-seven miles down the road from Niniltna, nine feet and three inches outside the Niniltna Native Association's tribal jurisdiction, and therefore not subject to the dry law currently in effect. Or was it damp? Kate thought it might have changed, yet again, at the last election from dry to damp, or maybe it was from wet to damp. It seemed like every time she checked her mail in Niniltna, either the Alaska Beverage Distributors or whatever passed at the moment for the local temperance league had someone standing outside the post office with a petition.

Kate couldn't understand it herself. The first time Niniltna passed a dry law—no liquor allowed to be owned or sold within tribal boundaries—alcohol-related crime dropped 87 percent the first month and Trooper Jim Chopin was made conspicuous by his absence, a consummation devoutly to be wished for, in Kate's opinion. When it went to damp at the next election—no one could sell liquor, but people could have it for private consumption in their homes—the stats went back up and Jim was more in evidence. When it went to wet—liquor allowed to be sold within tribal boundaries—incidents of child abuse, spousal abuse, assault, burglary, rape, and even murder all went through the roof and Jim spent more time in the Park than he did in Tok, where his post was based.

It was evident to Kate that booze made you stupid. If she could have made alcohol disappear by wishing it so, it would have vanished off the face of the entire planet. On the other hand, Bernie was a responsible bartender, who had been known to disable snow machines to keep drunks from driving home. She'd seen him refuse service to pregnant women, and Auntie Vi kept a running tally of who was and who wasn't to keep Bernie informed. If people have to drink, Kate thought, swinging out of Bernie's parking lot, Bernie's is the place I'd send them.

The last of the light had gone while she was inside. It was one of those rare clear winter evenings when it was warm enough to be outdoors, only three below by the thermometer nailed to the Roadhouse wall. The stars seemed to be in a contest to see which could shine the brightest, and Kate roared down the road, with Mutt up behind and the Pleiades overhead for company. One knee was balanced on the seat, the other leg braced on the running board, hands light on the handlebars. The wolf ruff of her parka made a frosty tunnel for her to look through, and the headlight showed a trail packed hard by truck tire, snow machine tread, and dogsled runner. The alder, birch, and spruce crowded in on either side, and once, a bull moose whose rack looked like it was about to fall off ambled onto the trail. She slowed, and he vanished into the brush opposite. She thumbed the throttle again.

Kate loved driving through the Arctic winter night. The snow, a thick, cold, unfathomable blanket swathing the horizon in every direction, reflected the light of the stars and the moon and the aurora so that it returned twicefold to cast the shadows of tree and bush in dark relief. On those nights, the Park seemed to roll out before her forever, a land of dreams, so various, so beautiful, so new. No darkling plain here, and never mind Matthew Arnold, whom Kate had always found to be a humorless grouch anyway.

The snow machine took a sudden dip in its stride. Mutt bumped into Kate but kept her balance.

At the top of a long slope that curved right, she slowed enough to take the turnoff. This trail was barely a rut between thick stands of spruce, and it required attention and a slow speed, so slow that Mutt grew impatient and hopped off to streak ahead, her plate-sized feet skimming over the surface.

A few minutes later, Kate pulled into a clearing and killed the engine. The rising moon lit a peaceful woodland scene right out of Laura Ingalls Wilder. A small log cabin perched on a precipitous hillside. The foundation was made of smooth gray rocks from the Kanuyaq River, overshadowed by a large deck that projected from the first floor, looking south. The roof was peaked and frosted with two feet of snow, through which a stovepipe chimney rose. A thick spiral of smoke curled from the top. Trees crowded around the eaves as if for comfort or, perhaps, to listen in on conversations that over the years had had much to do with them.

Two large picture windows set into the walls of the second floor were bright, lit from within. A long set of wooden stairs led to the deck, at the top of which there was a door, open. Against the light streaming out into the night, Kate could see a thin, stooped figure scratching Mutt's head. Mutt's tail was wagging hard enough to make her butt fall off, but there were no lavish kisses exchanged. Mutt was a strict heterosexual, even across species, and, save only Kate, an all-man dog.

"Come on up, Kate," a voice said. Kate killed the engine and climbed the stairs.

Inside, there was barely enough room to inhale, it was so crowded with furniture and stacks of papers, books, and magazines that one had to turn sideways to get from one side of the house to the other. An Earth stove radiated heat from the center of the room. An upright piano stood in another corner, piled high with sheet music. In a third corner was the kitchen, a counter with a small propane stove on it, a sink in it, and doorless cabinets above and below jammed with cans and bags. An aroma of savory stew lingered in the air, along with— Aha. A pie in a deep dish sat on the counter, perfectly browned and oozing dark red juice. A small square table was almost visible beneath an old manual typewriter, a ream of typing paper, and piles of what looked like legal documents and receipts. An enormous black cat looked out from her seat on one of the two upright wooden chairs shoved beneath the table and gave Mutt a perfunctory hiss, which Mutt regally ignored. Noblesse oblige.

Like Kate's cabin, this one had a loft for sleeping. The fourth corner was for living. Two comfortable-looking chairs and a small couch were within easy reach of a coffee table, a tired slab of ersatz wood covered with heel marks and glass rings and an overflowing ashtray.

Every available inch of wall space was given over to bookshelves, and every shelf was full. In the hissing light of the Coleman lanterns, it could be seen that the titles were organized alphabetically by author, and separated into fiction and nonfiction. With difficulty, Kate restrained from diving in headfirst. She shucked out of parka and bib overalls and took a seat on the couch. Mutt leapt up gracefully beside her and sat grinning at the woman in the chair opposite.

Dina Willner was thin to the point of emaciation, with sparse white hair pulled back into a severe knot at the nape of her neck. Her nose was large and hooked, her small, faded blue eyes narrow and fierce. She wore button-front Levi's and a blue plaid wool shirt, the elbows worn through to the light blue thermal underwear beneath. A cigarette was tucked into the corner of her mouth, smoke curling up to form a ragged halo around her head. Her cane, a twisted affair made of diamond willow and heavily varnished, leaned against the arm of her chair. Her pale pink fuzzy footwear had eyes and ears and whiskers. "I'm liking the bunny slippers, Dina," Kate said.

Dina raised a foot to regard it with satisfaction. "Nice, aren't they?"

"I'll have to get a pair for myself. Thanks, Ruthe." She accepted a heavy white mug of coffee.

Ruthe Bauman handed Dina a mug and settled into the other chair. "The stew'll be hot in about ten minutes."

"Caribou?" Kate said hopefully.

"Moose."

Kate smiled. Not bad for second-best. Life was good.

Ruthe was tall and slender, her hair a short mop of silky curls that had once been blond and were now a soft white gold that still clustered thickly around her face. Her skin was clear and pale, with crow's feet around her large brown eyes and laugh lines around her wide mouth. She wore khaki slacks, a pumpkin-colored sweater over a white turtleneck, and chunky white socks. The only thing spoiling the effect was the wood slivers and pine needles adhering to the soles of the socks.

Silence was not the enemy to these two women, and Kate sipped her coffee and thought about them.

Nobody in the Park knew how old they were, but everyone knew the legend. How Dina and Ruthe had flown for the WASPs during World War II, towing targets over the Atlantic Ocean for fighter pilots to practice on. How rumor had it that one of them had been the WASP pilot instructor Paul Tibbets had tapped to fly the new Boeing bomber, to shame the male pilots afraid to fly it into climbing into the cockpit. How, after the war, Dina and Ruthe had been unwilling to give up flying and in 1946 had come to Alaska in search of jobs in the air. How in 1947 they had teamed up with Arthur Hopperman of Hopper Holidays, a travel agency out of Fairbanks that specialized in guiding hunters and fishermen to record kills in the Alaska Bush. How in 1949 they had bought out Art, acquired two de Havilland Beavers, and started flying tourists into remote lodges in the Bush, pioneering eco-tourism before it was fashionable enough to merit the hyphen. How in 1951 they had bought this cabin and the surrounding eighty acres from a homesteader heading south for the last time and had proceeded to build another ten cabins farther up the hill, along with a bathhouse, a cookhouse, a mess hall, and a greenhouse, and had started flying tourists into Niniltna and putting them up at Camp Theodore, which they had named for Theodore Roosevelt.

That was a sign right there, all the Park rats said, and they waited grimly, rifles in hand, for Ruthe and Dina to start preaching conservation. They didn't have to wait long, and Ruthe and Dina didn't just preach it; they practiced it. "To leave as small a footprint as possible" was their declared and shameless intention. They grew their own food; they even had half a dozen apple trees that they actually managed to coerce into bearing fruit. They recycled paper. They had a compost heap. They avoided the use of plastic. They wouldn't allow hunting on their property, which, since it was only eighty acres, didn't amount to much of a statement, but then they started lobbying in Juneau and Washington, D.C., for stronger laws governing the taking of fish and game, and the disposal of human waste in the Bush, and the damming of rivers and streams for power, and the use of heavy equipment in gold mining. Most damning of all, they were personal friends of Jimmy Carter, who visited Camp Theodore at least once every year, and sometimes twice.

That alone should have been enough to ostracize them, to make and keep them bunny-loving, tree-hugging outcasts, but, like everything else, it wasn't that simple. Ruthe and Dina were too nice, too smart, too funny, too, well, just too damn *authentic*. Alaskans pride themselves on what makes them different from Outsiders, and, as Mac Devlin put it, "You don't get much different than a coupla old lesbos living way the hell and gone up a mountain, selling the view to a buncha tree huggers, and making a damn good living at it, too." "And how can you hate someone who was a WASP?" George Perry said. "They care about the land," Ekaterina Moonin Shugak said simply, and they were in.

One of Ruthe and Dina's first acts upon establishing Camp Teddy was to reach out to the local arm of the Alaska Native Sisterhood, of which Ekaterina Moonin Shugak was at that time president. The three strong women bonded instantly, forming a lifetime friendship, which was not lessened by Ekaterina's death. Ruthe and Dina made serious donations to the fund that supported the fight for the Alaska Native Claims Settlement Act in 1972. When Dina and Ruthe began agitating for the designation of the Park as an "International Biosphere Reserve," Ekaterina was first in line to demonstrate her support, which all by itself would have guaranteed its success.

Not coincidentally, Ruthe and Dina had also dandled Ekaterina's grandbaby, Kate, on their knees practically from the moment of her birth. Dina had instructed a nine-year-old Kate in the art of rappelling down a cliff face, after Ruthe had taught her how to get up it. Thanks to Ruthe and Dina, before Kate was twelve, she was on a first-name basis with every living thing in the Park, Animalia and Plantae, by division, class, order, family, genus, and species. Both women had taken her white-water canoeing on the Kanuyaq and saltwater kayaking on Prince William Sound. In this, they had Ekaterina's tacit, if not overt, approval, because in those days all it took for Kate to be against something was Ekaterina to be for it. The result was a greater understanding of the ecosystems among which she lived, and an appreciation of the whole of nature itself that would last her whole life long.

So, not unnaturally, when it came time to lobby for the Alaska National Interest Lands Conservation Act, also known as d-2, Park rats were unsurprised when the Niniltna Native Association, of which the same Ekaterina Moonin Shugak was then president and chief executive officer, lined up behind it. ANILCA created ten new national parks within the state, and added to four already existing parks, one of which had Camp Teddy smack in the middle of it.

The Park was now 20 million acres in size, located between the Quilak Mountains and the Glenn Highway on the north, the Canadian border on the east, Prince William Sound in the south, and, variously, the Trans-Alaska Pipeline, the pipeline haul road, and the Alaska Railroad on the west. It was drained by the Kanuyaq River, which twisted and turned over 225 miles in its search for the sea, coming to it in an immense delta east of Alaganik Bay, which saw the return each year of five species of Alaskan salmon in quantities capable of supplying tables in gourmet restaurants as far away as New York City, as well as the drying racks and smokehouses as far upriver as the creek behind Kate's cabin.

The river was navigable by boat in summer and by snow machine in winter. The coast was almost impenetrable everywhere else, defended by a lush coastal rain forest made of Sitka spruce, hemlock, alder, birch, willow, and far too much devil's club. Behind it, the land rose into a broad valley, then a plateau, foothills, and lastly the Quilaks, mountains forming an arc of the Alaska Range. There was a grizzly bear ("Of the Kingdom Animalia" went Dina's voice, starchy and schoolmarmy, "*Ursus arctos horribilis,* once known to roam much of the continent of North America, now restricted to the northern Rockies, western Canada, and, of course, Alaska") for every ten square miles, and following a good salmon year, even more. There were moose, white-tailed deer, mountain goats, Dall sheep, wolves, coyotes, wolverines, lynx, fox both arctic and red, beaver, marmot, otters, both land and sea, mink, marten, muskrat, and snowshoe hare. There were birds from the mighty bald eagle to the tiny golden-crowned sparrow, and every winged and web-footed thing in between.

The hand of man lay lightly here. There were a few good-sized towns, Cordova on the coast, Ahtna in the interior, both with about three thousand people, and maybe thirty villages ranging in population from 4 to 403. One road, a gravel bed left over a thriving copper mine in the early days of the last century, was graded during the summer but not maintained after the first snowfall. If you wanted to get somewhere in the Park, you flew. If you didn't fly, you took a boat. If the river was frozen over, you drove a snow machine. If you didn't have a snow machine, you used snowshoes. If you didn't have snowshoes, you stayed home in front of the fire until spring and tried not to beat up on your family. There were Park rats who disappeared into the woodwork in October and were not seen again until May, when it was time to get their boats out of dry dock and back into the water, but they were few in number and so determinedly unsociable that they weren't missed.

The Park, in fact, looked much as it had a hundred years before, even perhaps a thousand years before. That it did was at least in part due to the two old women now eating Ruthe's legendary moose stew across from Kate this evening. Kate finished first and got up to refill her bowl. "There's some spice in this I can't identify," she said, hanging over the cauldron on the back of the woodstove. She sniffed at the rising steam. "You don't put cloves in it, do you?"

"Good heavens, no," Ruthe said placidly, but Kate noticed she didn't volunteer what spice it was.

"You don't want the recipe to die with you," she said with intent to provoke.

Dina choked and had to be thumped on the back. She mopped her streaming eyes and said, "That's the first time I've heard that one, at least to Ruthe's face."

They finished their stew and moved on to coffee. "Like a piece of pie, Kate?" Ruthe said.

"Yes," Kate said, practically before Ruthe finished getting the words out of her mouth.

On top of everything else, Ruthe was an incredible cook.

She'd trained all the chefs hired for Camp Teddy. No visitor ever went home hungry. The coffee was terrific, too, a special blend made up by Kaladi Brothers, an Anchorage roaster. They called it the Ex-President's Blend. You couldn't buy it in stores. Kate had tried. She raised her mug, just to smell this time. It was coffee like no other, and Kate, an unabashed addict, was deeply appreciative. When she lowered the mug again, a thick wedge of pie was suspended in front of her. She was grateful there was a fork. She feared for her manners had there not been.

"Oh god, that was good," she said, using her finger to scoop up the last bit of juice. "What gives it that tangy taste on the back of the tongue? Rhubarb and what else? I've tried and tried at home to get that flavor, but I never quite succeed."

Ruthe grinned. "Trade secret."

Kate sighed, putting her heart into it. It had no effect, other than another snort of laughter from Dina and a refill of her mug from Ruthe. Kate sat back, trying to look as mournful as possible, which wasn't easy with a bellyful of Dinner by Ruthe.

"So what was it you wanted to talk to us about, Kate?" Dina said, lighting a new cigarette from the butt of the old one, and earning a reproving look from Ruthe, which got Ruthe precisely nothing.

Ruthe tucked herself neatly into the other recliner, looking like an advertisement for Eddie Bauer on a good day, and fixed Kate with an expectant look.

"I need your help."

"What with?"

"It seems Dan O'Brian is too green for the current administration, and he's being encouraged to take early retirement."

Dina and Ruthe exchanged glances. "Pay up," Dina said.

Ruthe sighed and unwound herself to fetch a smart brown leather shoulder-strap purse, from which she extracted a twenty-dollar bill and handed it over. Resuming her seat, she said in answer to Kate's raised eyebrow, "I bet they would hold their hand until the midterm elections. Dina said it'd be before."

"You mean you expected this?"

Ruthe's laugh was half in anger, half in sorrow. "After the last election, we put it on the calendar, Kate. There isn't a conservationist worthy of the name in the present cabinet. Look at what's happened just in the last twelve months."

"The Sierra Club comes out with a report that says all-terrain vehicles rip up the land," Dina said, and snorted out smoke like a dragon breathing fire. "Something we've been telling them for years, but they have to do their little studies. Hell, you've seen it yourself, jerks blazing trails all over the Park in spite of the prohibitions against it, and the federal government, the main landowner of the Park, of the state, when it comes down to it, exercises no authority."

"They don't have the manpower," Ruthe said softly.

Dina glared. "They don't have the manpower because the government won't allocate funds for proper oversight of the lands in their care. That doesn't stop the ruts the ATVs leave behind from diverting entire streams. Taiga and tundra both all torn to hell, habitat irreparably damaged." She pointed her cigarette at Kate. "I went with a Cat train up to Rampart in 1959, where that moron—what was his name? Oh, Teller, yeah. Well, Teller thought he was going to blast out a dam with a nuclear explosion. Five years ago, I flew to Fairbanks, and guess what? You can still see the track we left. From ten thousand feet up, Kate, you can still see it. Forty years ago, and it's still there. And don't even get me started on the snow machines."

Kate remembered the two drunks on snow machines who had invaded her front yard two springs ago. "I know."

"A lot of people need them for basic transport," Ruthe said. "And for hunting trips, and supply runs."

"A lot of people ride them straight up mountains to see

if they can get avalanches to fall on them, too," Dina snapped. "Which I call a self-correcting problem when they succeed, not to mention a triumph for the gene pool."

"Dina," Ruthe said. She didn't say, You don't mean that, but Kate could hear it all the same.

"And what does our absentee landlord do?" Dina said. "Nothing, that's what. And they're going to continue doing nothing, because if they started cracking down on every charter member of the NRA, it would send up a scream you could hear on Mars."

Kate didn't quite know how they'd made it from snow machines to gun control, but from long experience Ruthe had an answer. "I'm a member of the NRA," she said mildly. At Dina's glare, she added, "Keep your friends close, and your enemies closer."

Kate laughed, and then at Dina's glare turned the laugh into a cough.

"They want to drill for oil in ANWR," Dina said. "They want to punch some exploratory holes in Iqaluk. Of course they want to get rid of the rangers like Dan O'Brian, the ones who've been here for a while, the ones who don't just talk the talk. Never mind that Alaska is the last place in the nation, maybe even the last place on the planet, that still looks like it did in the beginning. Oh, yeah." She snorted smoke. "You bet. It's the rangers with practical experience on the ground who might actually have a clue as to how that would affect the wildlife who will be the first to go."

Kate turned to Ruthe, who looked ever so faintly apologetic. "Well," Ruthe said, her soft voice sounding the antithesis of Dina's harsh tones, "I'm not sure we shouldn't let them drill."

Dina sat straight up in her chair. "What!"

"With conditions." Ruthe's gaze was limpid. "They can drill in ANWR, if they keep their mitts off parks and refuges in the rest of the state."

Dina sat back, scowling ferociously at the possibility that Ruthe might have a point. "Like they'd agree to that."

"So far, we've got the votes," Ruthe said. "Unless they changed the Constitution when I wasn't looking, which these days seems more and more possible, every president still has to go through the United States Congress. That's a hundred senators and over four hundred representatives, each and every one with his or her own agenda and priorities. If we put this problem away for them, think how grateful they'll be."

"The Sierra Club and the rest of the gang will never go for it."

"Not right away, no. Eventually . . ."

There was a brief, telling silence. Kate wondered if she was watching policy being made.

"What do you think, Kate?"

Kate, jolted out of her reverie, said, "What?"

"Should we trade ANWR for the rest of the park lands?"

Kate tried to avoid the issue. "I don't live there."

"It's publicly owned land, Kate."

"Upon which Alaska Natives have been subsisting for millennia."

"And some of them are for drilling in ANWR."

Kate tried another tack. "Is there actually any oil there?"

Ruthe shrugged. "Nobody knows for sure. There's only been one well drilled there—by the state, I think—and they're keeping the results secret."

"Anybody guessing?"

"The last estimate I heard was enough to keep the nation running at full throttle for three months," Dina said.

"Really? That's all?"

"Some guessers say there's more than other guessers say."

Dina glared at her lifelong roommate. There was no way Kate was going to get in the middle of this. "About Dan O'Brian," she said.

"Oh yes, Dan," Ruthe said with quick sympathy, and perhaps relief. "How is he taking it?"

"He likes his job, he's good at it, and he doesn't want to leave the Park. He probably wouldn't anyway—he's in love again."

Ruthe gave Dina a smug look. "We noticed."

"Oh yeah?"

"Yes indeed. We were at the Roadhouse the night they met."

Dina blew out a cloud of smoke and watched it rise into the air. "It was one of the better seductions I have witnessed," she admitted. "I do so enjoy seeing a thing well done."

"What do you mean?" Kate said.

Dina stabbed the air with her cigarette, emphasizing her points. "Dan walked into the room, and that girl zeroed in on him like a heat-seeking missile. Target acquired, and— three, two, one—impact!"

Kate looked at Ruthe, who was laughing in spite of herself. "It was kind of like that," she admitted. "Poor Dan didn't stand a chance."

"Poor Dan isn't exactly yelling for help," Kate said. "And about Dan. What's the point of him just holding down a cabin when he's so much more useful at riding herd on Park rats shooting out of season and yo-yos flying in from Anchorage to shoot at everything that moves? He doesn't want to resign, but you know that if they're that determined, they'll find a way to force him out."

"What do you want us to do?"

Kate met Dina's fierce eyes and smiled. "I want you 'to do that voodoo that you do so well.' Make some calls. Call in some favors. Twist some arms if you have to. Get whoever is in charge down there to lay off Dan."

Ruthe met Dina's eyes, a smile in her own, and for a fleeting moment, the two old women looked eerily similar.

"Of course, if we do this for you," Dina said, "you'll owe us."

Kate took a careful breath. "I kind of thought the whole Park would owe you."

Dina stared down her eagle beak. "You thought wrong."

"Yeah." Kate sighed. "Okay. I'll owe you."

Dina cackled, then lit another cigarette.

Ruthe poured another round of coffee, this time with a shot glass of the framboise Dina made from their raspberry patch every fall. To be polite, Kate touched her lips to the glass and set it down again. They spent the next hour exchanging Park gossip. Dandy Mike had actually been dating the same woman for more than a month. The high school varsity basketball team, under Bernie's able coaching, was fourteen and three for the season, and Bernie was greatly torqued about the three. Anastasia Totemoff had died of ovarian cancer. "At least it was quick," Dina said, shifting in her chair, an expression of pain crossing her face. "Two weeks and she was gone."

"How is Demetri?" Ruthe said quickly.

"He's maintaining, but . . ." Kate shook her head.

"I don't know what Demetri's going to do with all those kids," Ruthe said.

"Raise them," Kate said. "I think there's only one left at home anyway."

Dina snorted cigarette smoke.

"Who's this Christie Turner?" Kate said. "Dan says she's been here since October. Today's the first time I've seen her."

"I hear," Dina said, bright eyes snapping maliciously, "that she's a professional gal out of Las Vegas."

"Oh, come on," Ruthe said. "Every woman who comes into the Park who looks halfway decent and who doesn't jump into bed with the first six guys who ask her is always branded as selling it to someone else. Honest to god." She cast up her eyes in disgust. "I'd say she'd worked her way up the AlCan waiting tables. She's pretty good."

"I don't like her," Dina said flatly.

Ruthe looked at her askance. "Why not?"

"Too pretty," Dina said. "Might cut in on our action." She cackled again.

One of Dan's rangers had apprehended an FBI agent and a police lieutenant from the Anchorage police department. They'd been shooting at moose out of season and without a license, and while on the outside of the better part of a half gallon of Calvert's, which had not improved their aim, as they had nearly taken out the ranger along with the moose. Since Anchorageites were the butt of most Park jokes, this incident had given rise to much merriment. The Kanuyaq caribou herd had topped 23,000 in population and was in danger of eating itself out of house and home. Since the herd migrated from its state land grazing area to its calving ground near the headwaters of the Kanuyaq in the Park, the Park Service had consulted with the state Fish and Game people and had come up with a plan to allow flying and shooting the same day, with a maximum take of five caribou per hunter, and they were even allowing each hunter to take one cow. "Beginning when?" Dina said with a gleam in her eye. She'd always been one of the best shots in the Park, and she was fond of saying that if she hadn't been, she and Ruthe would have starved to death those first years on their mountain.

"The first week of January," Kate said. "They want to wait until the males shed their racks, so we don't get a bunch of trophy hunters looking for something to put over the fireplace."

Ruthe groaned. "Forget about it. I'm not up to hunting this year." She fluttered her eyelashes. "Let's find some nice young hunk to bring home the bacon for us." They all laughed, but Kate was aware that Ruthe's recent disinclination to hunt had more to do with the sudden onset of

Dina's old age than it did with lack of interest. Over the past year, Dina had gone from being a vital woman in glowing health to an old woman with shaking hands and a shakier step. She walked only with the aid of her cane, and had to be helped from her chair, as if her back had lost all its strength. Her hands, once so strong and so capable, hands that had hauled Kate over the edge of a cliff by the scruff of her neck on more than one occasion, had deteriorated into shrunken claws. It hurt Kate to look at them, and so she didn't.

Billy and Annie Mike had adopted a Korean baby and named him Alexei, for Annie's grandfather. "My god," Dina said in disgust, "the woman had seven children of her own. Wasn't that enough?"

"Evidently not," Ruthe said.

Dina had the grace to look slightly ashamed. "Sorry," she said gruffly. "Never been a kid person."

"Yeah, you never could stand having me around," Kate said, and Ruthe laughed out loud.

Mandy and Chick were in training for the Yukon Quest. "Every day at noon, like clockwork," Kate said, "I hear dog howls coming down the trail. I open the door and to what to my wondering eyes should appear but Chick, stopping by for cocoa and fry bread."

Ruthe and Dina laughed. "Thinks with his stomach," Dina said. "What I call a proper man."

Ruthe refilled their mugs. "I saw John Letourneau putting the moves on Auntie Edna," Kate said, stirring in evaporated milk. The quality of the silence that followed her remark made her raise her head.

At her curious look, Dina said, "Yeah, I saw that, too," and added with a sneer, "He's probably after her for that property she owns on Alaguaq Creek."

"Oh, I don't know about that," Ruthe said immediately. "I think Auntie Edna has more than enough charm to explain John's interest."

"Charm, schmarm," Dina said. "That man never does anything without an ulterior motive."

"That's not true, Dina, and you know it," Ruthe said, this time with an edge to her voice.

Kate stepped in to defuse the tension a little, although she was intensely curious as to why it had sprouted up in the first place. "He got a little tangled up in your cane, Dina, there on the dance floor."

"He sure did, didn't he? Can't think how that happened." She looked sharply at Kate. "Didn't see you out there."

They must have left before the conga line, Kate thought. "I don't dance."

"Hell you don't. Many's the time I've seen you whooping it up at a potlatch."

"That's a different kind of dancing."

"And why not dance them all? Dancing's good for what ails you. Kick up your heels and it lifts your spirits."

"It's good for your soul," Ruthe said.

Kate mumbled something, but by now the two old women were on the warpath.

"How's Johnny?" Ruthe said.

Like everyone else in the Park, Dina and Ruthe had a vital interest in the well-being of Johnny Morgan, who had come to the Park to live following his father's death. It was natural for them to ask, as Johnny was Jack Morgan's son, and Jack had been Kate's lover. "He's fine," Kate said.

Dina fixed her with a penetrating eye. "How are you?"

"I'm fine, too." Even if she did still wince at the mention of Jack.

Dina's fierce eyes saw an uncomfortable amount. "Huh," she said, lighting another cigarette. "Miss him?"

Kate took a deep breath. "Every day," she managed to say.

"But you're learning to live with it."

"Yes."

"And without him," Ruthe said.

"Yes." If the joy she found in sunrise over a world without Jack Morgan in it was not as strong as it had once been, it was no one's business but her own.

"That Ethan Int-Hout still sniffing around?"

"I—"

"The boy's got the look of someone who knows his way around a bed, I'll give him that."

To her acute embarrassment, Kate felt herself turn a brilliant red.

"That might be none of our business, Dina," Ruthe said.

"Oh balls! Everything in this Park is our business," Dina said, and pointed her cigarette at Kate again. "Shit or get off the pot. It's not like there aren't men waiting around the block to step up if you'd look at them twice."

"I suppose," Kate said in a desperate bid for one-upmanship, "you would know."

Dina only cackled again. "You bet your ass, I would, sweetie. Whether I took 'em up on it or not." She looked at Ruthe and her eyes softened. "You bet I would."

Ruthe put her hand over Dina's.

Kate stood. "Time for me to mosey on home."

"Say hi to Johnny for us," Ruthe said. "I like him, Kate. He values his elders."

"He's been up here?" Kate said, surprised.

Ruthe chuckled. "On half a dozen occasions. Seems like old times."

"And give Ethan our love," Dina said, and cackled as Kate climbed back into her down overalls and parka and headed out the door.

3

The two gentlemen in question were both at her cabin when she got there. Mutt knocked Johnny off the doorstep and wrestled him across the snow, growling in mock anger. Ethan stood in the doorway, watching as Kate ran the snow machine into the garage. "I'll be in in a minute," she called, and after a moment she heard boyish laughter and fake growls fade as the cabin door was closed.

She topped off the snow machine's gas tank, checked the oil, looked at the treads. The ax needed sharpening, and so, too, it seemed, did the hatchet. She checked the rest of the tools hanging in neat rows from the Peg-Board while she was at it. The truck had been winterized and was parked as far out of the way as possible at the back of the garage. The woodpile was down to four cords, and although it had been a mild winter thus far, it wouldn't hurt to haul in a few more trees from the woodlot and replenish it. She visited the outhouse—plenty of toilet paper and lime—and the Coleman lantern hanging from the planter hook on the wall was almost full of kerosene.

It wasn't that she didn't want to see Ethan, and it wasn't

that she didn't want to spend time with Johnny. She just wasn't used to anyone waiting for her when she got home. She kicked the snow from her boots and stepped inside.

It was a cabin much like the one she had come from, twenty-five feet on a side, with an open loft reached by a ladder. The logs had been planked over with a light pine and were sanded smooth and finished. The ceiling was Sheetrocked and painted white, making the interior much lighter than that of many Bush cabins. There was a large picture window to the right of the door as you faced in, and another large window over the sink, to the left of the door. Both windows faced southwest.

There was an oil stove for cooking, a woodstove for heat, a small table that looked leftover from the fifties with a Darigold one-pound butter can sitting in the middle of it, stuffed with paper money and change. An L-shaped couch had been built into one corner, covered in blue denim that looked as if it had been pieced together from old Levi's. The kitchen counter held a shallow porcelain sink mounted with a pump handle; open cupboards above and below were filled with canned goods and sacks of flour, sugar, and rice. Shelves ran all around the walls, filled mostly with books, but there were also decks of cards, board games, and a cassette deck with tapes. A .30-06 rifle and a pump-action 12-gauge shotgun were cradled in a rack over the door, ready to hand, boxes of ammunition on a shelf nearby. There were no family pictures, although there was a large, thick photo album sitting on one shelf. A tiny ivory otter, perched on his hind legs, thick fur ruffled from the water, looked at the room through gleaming baleen eyes.

There was a basketball rolled into the crease of the couch, and a guitar hung from a hook next to the door, but otherwise the room was a reflection of someone who liked to cook, read, and listen to music. Someone self-contained, self-sufficient, content with her own company, having no need in her day-to-day life for a telephone, cable TV, or Net access.

Someone, perhaps, who placed a high value on the qualities of solitude and silence.

Every lantern was lit, and the kettle was steaming on the woodstove. Dirty dishes had been washed and put away in the cupboard and the counter swept free of crumbs. The loaves of bread from that morning's baking were wrapped in tinfoil and the kettle of last night's stew had been removed to the cooler on the porch outside the front door. The cushions on the couch were plumped up, the books on the shelves were lined up. The cassette tapes were stacked in neat piles, labels out. Except for on the guitar, there wasn't a speck of dust anywhere.

It wasn't that she wasn't a notorious neatnik. It wasn't that she didn't appreciate someone doing her chores for her. It was just that she was used to doing for herself. It made her inexplicably uneasy to be done for.

Still, she managed a smile for both man and boy. At face value, they were both well worth it. Ethan looked like a Viking, tall, broad-shouldered, long-limbed, pale skin, blond hair, blue eyes; his forebears could have come from anywhere so long as anywhere was Norway, Sweden, or Denmark. Johnny was at that ungainly stage of adolescence when his limbs were growing out beyond his control, but he would be tall, too. He bore a striking resemblance to his father, thick dark hair over a heavy brow, deep-set blue eyes, firm mouth, strong chin. He would never be handsome, but his face, once seen, would never be forgotten.

"Hey," she said, shrugging out of her parka.

"Hey," Ethan said, catching it and leaning down to kiss her at the same time.

Johnny was sitting at the table, hunched over a book, and Kate instinctively pulled back. Ethan maintained his smile, but there was a frown at the back of his eyes. "Had dinner?"

"Yeah, I had dinner up to Ruthe and Dina's."

Ethan's lips pursed in a long, low whistle. "Lucky girl. They have pie?"

"Rhubarb and something extra."

"I'm jealous."

"It was good," Kate admitted. She pulled her bibs down and hung them next to the parka. The coat hook was crowded with Johnny's and Ethan's parkas and bibs, and hers were elbowed onto the floor. She picked them up and jammed them on the hook again. This time, they stayed.

"I was about to make some cocoa."

"I'd like that. It was a long ride home."

Ethan turned to the kettle. "What were you doing up at the old gals' place?"

"I went there to ask them to help with Dan."

"Ah." He was silent for a moment, measuring cocoa and honey and evaporated milk into three mugs. "I wasn't expecting you to charge off that way this morning when I came galloping over with the news."

Kate raised one shoulder. "He's a friend."

"Um." He brought her a mug. It had miniature marshmallows in it. She repressed a shudder.

He gave a second mug to Johnny, who grunted a thank-you without looking up, and came back to sit next to where she was curled up on the couch. He stretched out his long legs and propped his feet on the burl-wood coffee table, about the only piece of furniture in the room that had any pretension to style. "What did Dina and Ruthe have to say?"

"Well, they weren't surprised. They said the current administration wants to drill for oil in the Arctic, and it follows that they—the administration—will try to get rid of every bureaucrat who thinks otherwise."

"They don't have the votes in Congress, do they?"

"Ruthe says they don't." Kate tried to drink some cocoa without allowing her lips to come into contact with the marshmallows. It wasn't easy. "But I don't think she or

Dina have a lot of confidence that the situation is going to stay that way."

"You for it or against it?"

"What? Drilling in ANWR?" Kate thought about it. "I don't know. I've gone back and forth on it. I've been to Prudhoe Bay; they did a good job there. Then I think of *Valdez,* and how badly they did there. And then I think—" She stopped.

"What?"

"Well . . . well, it's just that maybe, once in a while, we should let a beautiful thing be, you know?" She looked at him. "What else is left like that?" She looked at Johnny, still hunched over his homework. "What do we leave behind when we're gone if we move into it now with D-nines?"

Ethan finished his chocolate. "I'm for it."

"You're for drilling?"

"Yeah. There'll be jobs, Kate. It's easy for you to say let it be, but I've got kids to support and educate."

"Your father raised four sons single-handedly before there was an oil patch."

"I'm not my father."

They were both angry, both aware of it, and both made a conscious decision to pull back from that anger. Ethan leaned forward to place his mug on the coffee table. "Where'd you get this table, anyway?"

"Buck Brinker made it for Emaa," she said. "I brought it home when she died."

"Thought I recognized the work. Nice piece."

"I like it. What did you do today?"

"Chopped wood."

"Filled up your woodshed?"

"Nope." He stretched, his joints popping, and gave her a lazy grin. "Filled yours."

"Oh. Ah. Well. Thanks."

"Thank me later."

She gave Johnny's back a warning glance.

Ethan's grin faded. "We've got to talk about this, Kate."

"Not now."

"It's always 'Not now.' When?"

Johnny sat up and closed his book with a decisive thump. "There!" He swiveled in his chair. "Done!" He fixed Kate with a hopeful eye.

"What?" she said.

He looked at the guitar.

So did she. Dust lay over it like a shroud.

"You said you would," Johnny said.

"I know I did," Kate said, reflecting on the unwisdom of making promises to adolescents. They were worse than elephants. It never occurred to her to renege, though. She set her mug next to Ethan's and got to her feet, ignoring the stifled sigh she heard Ethan give.

The guitar was an old Gibson that had belonged to Kate's father, who had left it behind when he died, along with an extensive collection of folk songs from the fifties, some with musical notation, some with only the chords penciled in over the stanzas, some just with the lyrics scribbled on a page torn from a school notebook. Collected in a black three-ring binder so old that the plastic cover was peeling away from itself, they were as foreign to Johnny as Bach was to Kate. She got the binder down and opened it on the coffee table, motioning Johnny to her side.

"Well," Ethan said with a lightness that was obviously forced, "I'm heading for home. See you back at the house, Johnny."

"Yeah," Johnny said.

"Or he can sack out here on the couch," Kate said. "Our Jane DEW line hasn't gone off in a while, so it should be safe." Jane was Johnny's mother and Jack's ex-wife, and a roaring bitch into the bargain. The good news was that she hated Kate with every part and fiber of her being. The bad news was she was trying to find her son in Kate's keeping so she could charge Kate with kidnapping.

All this stemmed from Johnny's father's death the pre-vious year. Jane had taken Johnny to Arizona to live with her mother, who was seventy-three and lived in a retirement community. Johnny had hated Arizona, hated the retire-ment community, and had nothing in common with his grandmother, who was into golf in a major way and who had considered her child-rearing days over once she got Jane out of the house. One morning, he'd put a couple of peanut butter sandwiches, a liter bottle of Coke, and a copy of *Between Planets* into his knapsack, swiped forty bucks out of his grandmother's purse, and hitched a ride on a semi loaded with lettuce. A Volkswagen van full of antiglobali-zation activists took him as far as Eugene, where he hooked up with a defrocked cop who was moving to Coeur d'Alene and who dropped him in Spokane. He walked across the border under the noses of Canadian immigration, hitched a ride on a U-Haul van full of furniture belonging to a family whose man was transferring from RPetCo Lima to RPetCo Prudhoe Bay, the driver of which was looking for a free ride to Alaska and didn't mind having company to keep him awake during the thousand-mile-plus journey. He dropped Johnny at the entrance to the Park on his way down the Glenn Highway to Anchorage. Johnny walked the rest of the way, appearing on Kate's doorstep tired, angry, and determined to stay.

Kate, who had weaseled the story out of him one leg at a time, was surprised that her hair hadn't turned white in the telling. Before she had time to formulate a plan, Jane had showed up in the Park, looking for Johnny. A Park rat who had no love for Kate had pointed Jane toward Kate's homestead, and Jane had materialized on the doorstep, breathing fire and smoke. Mutt had gotten rid of her for the moment, but she had legal custody of Johnny, and now she knew where Kate lived. She didn't know Ethan, how-ever, nor did she know where he lived, and since Ethan's wife had walked out on him and he had room and practice as a father of two, Kate had worked out an arrangement whereby Johnny lived for the most part on Ethan's homestead, safely out of Jane's reach, for the time being at least. This arrangement had the tacit, if not overt, sanction of the law, in the form of Trooper Jim Chopin. Ergo, Johnny was currently on the lam and the entire Park was in on the conspiracy to keep him that way until he was of age and could legally tell Jane to take a flying leap.

"Whatever," Johnny said, turning the pages of the notebook.

Not that he seemed overly worried about it.

He squinted at Stephan's writing. "Who's Woody Guthrie, Kate?"

Kate didn't want to look up, but she felt it would be cowardly not to. Ethan nodded at the door, his mouth set in a determined line. "I'll be right back," she said to Johnny.

"Yeah," he said again. He picked up the guitar, leaving fingerprints in the dust. He sneezed once, and a second time, and got up to dampen a dishcloth in the sink.

She shrugged into her parka and followed Ethan outdoors. His snow machine was parked to one side of the clearing, next to Johnny's. "How long is this going to go on, Kate?"

She gave a craven thought to saying, How long is what going to go on? but then thought better of it. Ethan's expression was very clear in the moonlight. "I'm just—I'm a little—I don't know, uncertain."

"What's this uncertain? You want me; I want you. I'm here, so are you. Jesus, Kate, this is just like college all over again."

Her head came up. " 'Just like college?' Who you going to sleep with instead of me this time, Ethan?"

He blew out an explosive breath. "That's not what I meant."

Anger was a good refuge. She thought about ducking

into it for maybe ten seconds. "I know," she managed to say.

"We've been dancing around sleeping together for, what, three months now?"

"No," she said in a low voice. "I've been dancing around it."

"Well," he said. "Okay." His smile flashed again.

She smiled in return, relieved. "I'm sorry, Ethan. It just hasn't felt right. I'm not ready. I don't jump into these things."

"Jack must have been one hell of a guy in the sack."

"It's not that," she snapped.

"I know," he said. "I'm sorry. I'm a little edgy around you."

She shoved her hands into the parka's pockets. "I'd better get inside."

"Hold it." He stepped forward to pull her into his arms and kiss her. He raised his head. "Feel that?"

Her response was instinctive, her legs opening a little to cradle him between them. "Who wouldn't?"

He kissed her again, this time with enough force to press her up against the cabin wall. He kneed her legs apart and rubbed himself between them. "I've wanted you for nearly twenty years. Jack is dead. Margaret left me. There's no reason not to. Unless you don't want to."

"It's not that. I—oh." His hand had worked its way inside her parka, and she arched into his hand. This was Ethan, high school heartthrob, very nearly her first lover. He was smart, he was funny, and, above all, he was capable, a quality she had always found irresistible in men. If his voice wasn't as deep as Jack's had been, as rough-edged in its desire, well, he wasn't Jack.

No one was.

He kissed her again. But he sure as hell could kiss. When he raised his head, her lips were swollen, her head was buzzing, and her knees were weak. And the smug grin on his face told her that he knew it. "More of that where it came from," he said, straddling his snow machine. "One bedroom over."

She stayed where she was, leaning up against the cabin for support, as he raised a hand and roared off into the night.

Back inside, she hung up her parka and worked the pump to fill up a pitcher of cold, clear water from the well located directly beneath the cabin. The well, fed by the water table created by the creek out back. Yet another example of her father's foresight and ability on this property he had homesteaded before she was born, like the handmade cabin and outbuildings, made of logs carefully fitted together, and as carefully chinked with moss and mud. Stephan Shugak had finished the inside of the cabin the same way, working a winter in Ahtna for a builders' supply company in exchange for insulation, Sheetrock, and nails, and the hammer to pound them in with. He had sanded the wall paneling by hand after cutting the planks from carefully selected trunks of Sitka spruce that he had felled himself on Mary Balashoff's setnet site on Alaganik Bay.

It had taken him six years to finish the job; in the process, he had sweated out the last of the memories from the months he had spent in the Aleutians as one of Castner's Cutthroats. When the last nightmare of the hand-to-hand combat on the beaches of Attu had faded into an uneasy memory, he had judged himself able to take a wife. He chose Zoya Swensen, a lithe woman of his own age, whose family came from Cordova, but like his had originated in the Aleutians, relocated first to Old Harbor on Kodiak Island and from there to Cordova where, it must be said, the first generation of expatriates complained bitterly of the warm climate.

Zoya and Stephan had wanted a house full of children, and instead they got Kate, just about the time they had given up hope of any children at all. This might have explained why first Zoya and then Stephan began drinking. Or it might not. They died so early in Kate's life that there was much she didn't know about them. She remembered her father more than she did her mother. He'd taught her to hunt, to use tools to construct and repair buildings and machinery, to chop wood, and to fish. They had built a wooden skiff together, more or less, in the garage the winter she turned five. He'd gotten two bears that winter, too, and they'd tanned the skins.

He hadn't taught her anything about love. Neither had Abel, Ethan's father, her guardian after Stephan died. That, she was still struggling to figure out on her own.

A mirror hung on the wall over the sink, and the grave woman reflected there, with the narrow, tilted hazel eyes and the very short dark hair beginning to go a little shaggy around the edges looked tired. Her summer tan had faded, too, leaving her skin looking sallow and stretched over her high cheekbones. Her wide mouth was unsmiling, a tight-lipped line of repudiation and denial. Ruthe and Dina had made that woman laugh. When was the last time she had laughed out loud?

A discordant jangle interrupted her reverie, and she looked over at the couch to see a frustrated expression on Johnny's face. "Here," she said, crossing the room and extending a hand. "I'll show you."

The guitar was in serious need of tuning, and she got out the tuning fork. It was a tedious process, but Johnny stuck with it. Afterward, she took him through the C and G chords, threw in a little practice on B7 just to keep things interesting. He liked the song "Scotch and Soda," and she located the Kingston Trio tape and played it for him so he'd know how it was supposed to sound. She tried him on "Where Have All the Flowers Gone," but although he liked the tune, he made a face at the lyrics. "Blowin' in the Wind" was okay, and so was "The Wreck of the Edmund Fitzgerald," which he misplayed with gusto.

"Okay, enough," Kate said at nine o'clock. "You going to Ethan's or you bunking here?"

"Here," he replied, which meant she didn't have to roll out the Arctic Cat again to follow him home, and she was grateful. She made more mugs of cocoa with Nestlé's, evaporated milk, and hot water from the kettle, but no marshmallows.

"My fingers hurt," he said.

She took his left hand and looked at the tips of his fingers. They were red and felt warm to the touch. "If you keep it up, they'll hurt worse. And then you'll work up calluses and they won't hurt anymore."

Unexpectedly, he took her left hand and looked at the tips of her fingers. "You don't have any."

"Not anymore."

"Because you quit playing."

"Yeah."

"Why?"

"I couldn't sing anymore, so there didn't seem to be much point."

His eyes went to her throat, to the scar that bisected it almost from ear to ear. "Because of that?"

"Yeah."

"How did you get it?"

"A guy had a knife. I took it away from him."

"But he cut you before you did."

"Yeah."

"When you were working for Dad."

"Yes."

"Does it still bother you?"

"The scar, or not being able to sing?"

"Both."

"Both," she replied, "although not as much as they used to." She put down the mug and picked up the guitar from where it was leaning against the coffee table. The weight of the body on her thigh felt familiar and unfamiliar at the same time, and the neck settled into her left palm with a tentative feeling. She gave the strings a few experimental strums, and without stopping to think about it, launched into "Molly Malone." Mutt, stretched out on the bearskin in front of the woodstove, raised her head, her ears going up, and fixed Kate with a steady gaze.

Kate's voice sounded husky to her hypercritical ears and she had to change octaves to hit the high notes. "Yesterday" was even harder to reach, but when she came to the end of the last verse, Johnny said, "That sounded fine. You can sing, Kate."

Her fingertips were tingling. She stood up and hung the guitar on its hook next to the door, making a mental note to oil the wood before Johnny's vigorous playing split the instrument in half. She looked over at Mutt, who had lowered her head back to her paws and appeared dead to the world.

"Can I learn to do that?"

"You can learn to do just about anything," Kate said. "It takes practice, is all."

He was about to reply, when a yawn split his face. She fetched sheets, blankets, and a pillow, and, in that unnerving fashion of adolescents, he was asleep before she smoothed the blankets over him. Shadows gathered as she turned off three of the kerosene lanterns, turning down the one hanging in the kitchen corner to leave a soft, dim glow in case he needed to get up in the middle of the night. Shadows moved with her across the floor and on the walls.

The book Johnny had been reading was a history textbook. School wasn't in session for another week. Kate sighed. Johnny was studying as hard as he could because it was his avowed intent to pass his GED when he turned sixteen, thereafter to walk away from school and never go back. She was hoping against hope that he'd fall in love with a girl whose avowed intent was to graduate high school in four years and go on to college afterward.

She stoked the fire in the woodstove, checked the oil stove to see that the pilot light was still burning, and refilled the wood box. After brushing her teeth and washing her face with the last of the water in the kettle, she refilled the kettle and set it on the back of the stove. She climbed the ladder to the loft and lit the lamp that hung next to the bed, undressing by its light, pulling on a nightshirt, and sliding beneath the thick down comforter. She was rereading *My Family and Other Animals* for what was probably the twenty-seventh time, but she had only lately gone back to full-time reading, and for the present, her preference was for books she had already read and enjoyed, ones with no surprises in them.

But even ten-year-old Gerry Durrell and his scorpions in matchboxes couldn't keep her attention this night. She put the book down and turned off the light to stare at the ceiling.

Jack Morgan had been dead for over a year now. She missed him, missed having him in her life. She missed his voice, she realized suddenly, that slow, deep bass voice that had made every feminine nerve she had stand up and salute every time she'd heard it.

Ethan's voice wasn't as deep, but that wasn't necessarily enough to deny the man her bed.

Jack had been brawny, a bruiser with the muscles of a prizefighter and a face that could most kindly have been described as interesting.

Ethan could have made a living modeling clothes for Brooks Brothers.

Only now did she realize how patient Jack had been, how long-suffering, how much he had put up with. When she had left Anchorage six years before, fresh out of the hospital, unable to form words clearly for four months—never mind sing—she had left the job and the man at one and the same time, vowing never to return to either. Eighteen months later, Jack had showed up in the Park with an FBI agent in tow and a missing person's case in hand. Eighteen months, during which she had tried to find his substitute in two other men, to no avail, both of whom she had made sure Jack knew about. If it had bothered him, he had never shown it. Much. He had waited for her—waited for her to heal, waited for her to come back to him—like he'd taken a vow to the Church of Kate Shugak and would not allow himself to become apostate.

He'd irritated her, bewildered her, astounded her, and charmed her. He had wooed her with Jimmy Buffett and seduced her with chocolate chip cookies, and in the end, he had saved her life at the expense of his own. "I love you, Shugak" had very nearly been his last words to her, and it was only after his death that she realized what they had meant.

She ached for him, suddenly, fiercely. They had been well matched sexually, coming together like thunder and lightning. She ran her hands down her body, remembering.

No. There was a perfectly good man not ten miles away. Why was she hesitating? Jack was dead, she was needy, and Ethan was eager. Love would never come again unless she gave it a chance. Wasn't that the way it worked? What was the matter with her?

She gave up on sleep, got up and dressed again, and crept down the ladder. Johnny didn't move. Mutt was waiting for her. She opened the door and slipped outside, catching it before the spring slammed it shut.

The trail around the cabin led to the A-shaped stack of six fuel drums. A fainter trail branched off from it and led through the trees, emerging at a cliff's edge. The boulder at the edge was as high as her waist, with a cleared spot on it worn smooth, just the size of someone's butt. Mutt sat at its foot, her shoulder at Kate's knee.

Below the snow-covered landscape was a crystalline palace, and above the stars seemed even brighter than they had before. The moon had a big smudged white ring around it that filled up half the sky. The northern lights were out, though only faintly and without much movement or color to them, long pale streaks across the northern horizon.

She'd turned thirty-five in October, and had been a sovereign nation unto herself pretty much from the age of six. It wasn't like she needed a man in her life. It was a matter of simple biology. And after all, she was Kate Shugak—she recognized no rules but her own. She could be chaste. Chaste by choice, by god, even Chaste by Choice—she could start a movement. Everything she wanted, everything she needed, it was all right here on this homestead. She had even, she reminded herself with awful sarcasm, managed to have a child without ever having given birth or having changed a single diaper. Now there was a miracle of modern parenting for you.

She could still feel the imprint of Ethan's mouth, hand, body. She could still taste him. How long had it been?

Somewhere very far away, or perhaps quite close, a songbird gave forth with three pure descending notes. Kate's laugh was half sob. "Oh, Emaa," she whispered, leaning her head on her knees, "these white boys are going to be the death of me. Where have all the Aleut boys gone, long time passing?"

Unbidden, the memory of those few moments in that bunk in Bering in July flashed into her head, and Jim Chopin's muffled curse rang in her ears. And later, the gentleness of his hands and lips and the—she could only call it the *kindness* in his eyes, the comfort of his arms just before he flew back to the Park.

"No," she said, jumping to her feet. Mutt, ears tuned to the rustle of a ptarmigan beneath a spruce tree thirty feet east, leapt up and barked an inquiry.

"No, no, *no*," Kate said, and marched back to the cabin.

4

Jim Chopin had been an Alaskan state trooper for almost twenty years, most of it posted in Tok, a town of twelve hundred, which sat on pretty much the northern limit of the Park and sixty-odd miles short of the Canadian border. The Tok trooper post, consisting of one sergeant and two corporals, constituted the sum of state law enforcement for the entire Park, a vast area occupied by less than fourteen thousand people—Park rats and Park rangers, hunters and trappers and fishermen, homesteaders, a few farmers, pilots, miners. They were elders and babies, housewives and career women, doctors, lawyers, and thirty-four Indian chiefs. They were white and Athabascan and Aleut and Tlingit and Eyak. They were Latino and Russian and Japanese and Korean. There was even one lone Frenchman from Toulouse, who had emigrated twenty years before and now had a cushy job pushing the grader down the road for the state, stationed at the road-maintenance facility at the Nabesna turnoff, from which he lay ardent siege to every woman with car trouble who drove or didn't drive by. His optimism was much admired, although even the cynical had to admit his success ratio was amazingly high. "Of course his standards aren't," Bernie pointed out, and sage heads nodded around the bar.

Jim, an immigrant from San Jose, California, liked two things about the Park right away: Pretty much everyone knew everyone else, and the air was clear every day. Later, when he passed his check rides, he liked flying even more, so much so that after getting his license for fixed wing, he went on ahead and got it for rotor, as well. Responding to a cry for help a hundred miles away and getting there in under an hour while never, ever, being stuck in traffic added considerably to the bottom line of his "Closed Cases" column.

He liked the people, good people, mostly, although obstinate, opinionated, determined, capable, and, above all, independent, with the highest per capita ratio of Libertarians in the state. Of course, this was a state where the Democratic party had feared that Jimmy Carter was going to come in third in the 1980 election.

He liked the sheer beauty of the place, the mountains, the rivers, the valleys. He liked that he could fly hundreds of miles in every direction with only an occasional roof, painted dark green to blend in with the treetops, to remind him that he was still on the same continent he'd been born on.

He liked the job. He knew he was good at it. He was the first call for the village elder with a knifing on his hands, the first call for the mayor of the town with the sniffing problem at the high school, the first call for the Fish and Game trooper who had caught someone fishing behind the markers. He knew where all the dope growers lived and where all the dealers they sold to drank, and who took the black bear out of season and sold the parts on the black market to what Asian dealers, and what guides were likely to violate the wanton-waste law by taking the rack and leaving the meat. He was all the law many of the Park rats would ever see in their lives, and for some of them, the only government representative. In his time, he had helped kids fill out Social Security forms, flown the public health nurse into villages where the entire student body of the local school had been stricken with chicken pox, backed up a tribal policeman in way over his head in a hostage situation involving a drunk, the drunk's best friend, the drunk's wife, a pint of Everclear, and a .357. Most of the time, he was able to talk the situation into the clear. A few times, he'd had to pull his weapon. So far, he had never had to fire it, managing to restrain himself under the grossest possible provocation, such as someone shooting at him first.

He was on call twenty-four/seven and the ringing of the phone sounded to his ear like a bugler sounding a charge. He was the cavalry riding to the rescue of any Park rat who was under attack, and he didn't care how politically incorrect the analogy was.

The phone rang constantly that morning in his office as he fielded calls from an irate father whose daughter had run off with her high school sweetheart, a distraught grandmother whose grandson had been beating her, a village elder reporting a shipment of 102 cases of vodka and whiskey into a dry village, a big game guide wanting to know what the summons was for and how the hell he was supposed to get to Ahtna for a courtroom appearance with his plane broken down. The next call was from a young man who had failed at fishing in Alaganik and who now wanted to go to the University of Alaska Interior in Ahtna to learn how to work a computer but didn't know how to fill out the form. Jim ascertained that the eloping daughter was of legal age, dispatched one corporal to take the grandmother's statement, dispatched another to intercept and confiscate the shipment of alcohol, hung up on the big game guide, and walked the fisherman through the application form.

The next call was from his boss in Anchorage. "Hey, Jim, how's it hanging?"

Jim sat back and put his feet up on his desk, there to admire the immaculate shine on his black leather boots. "About six inches from the floor," he replied.

A scoffing laugh. "Yeah, you wish."

"No, you do."

There followed the traditional exchange of insults and exaggerations so dear to the hearts of the male of the species, particularly those who were longtime friends and allies in the war on crime. Finally, his boss said, "We've been doing some thinking down here, Jim."

Uh-oh. "Thinking about what?"

"About your workload."

"What about it?"

A genial chuckle. "It's kind of heavy, isn't it?"

"So what else is new?"

"Well, we were thinking of lightening it up a little."

Jim took his feet off the desk and sat up to look at the map of the Park tacked to the wall behind his desk. "Define 'lightening up.'"

Another chuckle. "Breaking a chunk off your post's area of jurisdiction, for starters."

"What chunk?"

"The southern half. From, say, Niniltna south."

Fully half of his command. Which wouldn't do his career a hell of a lot of good. But then, he wasn't bucking for promotion anyway. He had no ambition to retire in Talkeetna.

On the other hand, he and his people were getting the job done. "What brought this on?"

A sigh. "You know we've got these bean counters running around down here right now, looking over our shoulders."

The Outside auditors the state had brought in. "I've heard."

The chuckle was not quite as genial this time. "Yeah. They've seen the amount of reports you file, the case load. They're thinking you're overworked, and that it's going to cause problems down the road."

"Why not just assign me another corporal?"

"I suggested that."

"And?"

"They also looked at the response times. Hell, Jim, they've got a point. That's the hell of a lot of territory you people cover. Some of that territory is a long way from where you're sitting."

Jim sat back and propped his feet on the windowsill this time, looking at the map of the Park. Niniltna was at its heart, when Ekaterina Moonin Shugak was still alive in more ways than one. Ahtna and Cordova were bigger, but Niniltna had the strong native association, with its solid leadership, and some legendary figures as shareholders. One in particular.

It also had a 4,800-foot airstrip, long enough to land a jet on—a small one anyway. Always supposing any pilot worthy of the name would put anything other than a Herc down on gravel. "Just as a matter of curiosity," Jim said, "have we got enough funding to create a new post?"

"Yeah, right."

A brief silence as Jim surveyed the map again. "Gene," he said, "are you satisfied with my work?"

A snort this time. "If I wasn't, you would have heard so before now."

"So if I come up with another way to set what passes for the bean counters' minds at ease, you'd listen to it?"

"Hell yes. What is it?"

"Give me a couple of days?" He waited.

"Yeah," Gene said finally. "Okay."

"One more thing."

"What?"

"You know Dan O'Brian?"

A brief pause. Jim could hear the Rolodex between his boss's ears clicking. "Dan O'Brian. Right. Chief ranger your area. What about him?"

"He mouthed off about drilling for oil in ANWR. They're trying to force him into retirement."

"So? Should have kept his mouth shut."

"Agreed, but otherwise he's a good man. We work well together. I'd hate to have to break in some newbie. Can you call somebody, make some noise?"

"I can call several."

"I owe you."

"Maybe. Maybe not. We'll see after the next time we talk."

"Gotcha," Jim said, grinning. He hung up, and grabbed his jacket and hat on his way out the door.

It was as clear and calm this morning as it had been the night before, the big high pressure system hanging over interior Alaska strong enough to keep it that way for the next three to four days. He had done preflight and refueled the Cessna with the shield on its side the night before. All he had to do was roll her out, and he was in the air five minutes later. He was on the ground in Niniltna in less than an hour, taxiing up to the hangar that served as headquarters for George Perry's two-plane air taxi service. George was there, pulling the backseat from his Super Cub and loading the back with mailbags. "Thank God for the U.S. Postal Service," he said in greeting.

A U.S. Postal Service mail contract had been the savior of more than one Bush air taxi running on duct tape and the owner's sweat. "What's with all the packages going out?"

George grinned. "Christmas returns."

"Oh." The only Christmas presents Jim sent were to his parents, usually something out of a catalog. In return, he got a card accompanied by a baseball cap with the logo of whatever sports team his father was currently following, and a box of his mother's homemade fudge. The fudge, he ate immediately. The cap usually went to the first kid he saw in the next village he flew into. The card lasted longer than either of them.

"What's up?" George said. "Somebody get uppity enough to require the personal attention of the law?"

Jim gave a noncommittal grunt. George had heard that grunt before, and he changed the subject. "See you at Bernie's later?"

"I don't know. Depends on if I have to make a run."

"Try." George grinned. "I hear somebody made a successful winter assault on Big Bump."

"Ah. It's Middle Finger time."

"You got it."

"George?"

"What?"

"Tell me about weather in the Park."

George cocked a quizzical eyebrow.

"Pilot to pilot," Jim said.

George's take was that it was typical Interior weather—a lot of cold, clear days in the winter and a lot of hot, clear days in the summer, if you didn't count the blizzards and the forest fires, respectively. "We're in between the Alaska Range and the Chugach Range," George told him, "with the Quilaks at our backs, and we're far enough away from all of them to keep us CAVU more often than not. So what's all this about?"

"Something in the wind," Jim said. "I'll let you know."

"Will it be good for the air taxi business?"

"Yes. In fact, start figuring out how much you'd charge to haul prisoners to Ahtna, Tok, or Anchorage. And try to keep it below highway robbery."

"Wilco." George, not the most curious of men, tossed the seats in on top of the mail and cut the conversation short. "Gotta go. Got three passengers waiting on a ride into the Park, and it ain't so often this time of year I got a full load coming back from a mail run."

George took off and Jim walked around the hangar and down the road. His destination wasn't far, but then, nothing in Niniltna was far from anything else. A block in that direction was the school, a block in the other the river, and in between was the airstrip and the mostly handmade homes of the town. The Niniltna Native Association building, prefabricated, vinyl-sided, and tin-roofed, stood on its own ground a little farther out and a little higher up, looking like a benevolent uncle with a fat belly, kicking back in the winter sunshine.

Ekaterina Moonin Shugak had ruled her kingdom from there. In her titular place was now Billy Mike, the association's new president and tribal chief. But through a long and profitable acquaintance with the Park and all its residents, Jim knew where the real power lay.

He went to see Auntie Vi.

Auntie Vi lived in a big house that used to be filled with children and was now filled with guests who paid far too much for a bed, a bathroom down the hall, and an unvarying breakfast of cocoa and fry bread. It was good cocoa, Hershey's, homemade, and superb fry bread, and Jim was lucky to be early enough to be offered some of both. He sat down next to a man in a nattily stitched denim pantsuit. The man took one look at Jim's uniform and ate the rest of his meal with as much of the back of his head toward Jim as possible, and then sidled out at his earliest opportunity.

"A uniform does have a way of clearing out a room," he said ruefully to Auntie Vi.

She laughed as she finished clearing the table. "This way, I didn't have to serve him seconds. Ay, those bums, they eat me out of house and home if they have the chance."

Just then, her other guests came in, a couple of state surveyors, who conversed in numbers, scribbling lines and formulae on a sheet of paper held between them. Jim wasn't sure they'd even registered his existence. They left, too, after stuffing themselves and their pockets with fry bread, which immediately showed up in grease stains on the outsides of their jackets. Jim noticed Auntie Vi made no objection, and he reflected on the state's propensity not to dicker on a set price for Bush accommodation. Auntie Vi's favorite customer, the state of Alaska.

Auntie Vi was about four feet tall and weighed maybe eighty pounds with her false eyelashes on. She was one of Ekaterina's contemporaries and therefore had to be in her late seventies, if not her early eighties, but the years sat lightly upon her shoulders. She had her share of wrinkles around the eyes and mouth and the backs of her hands, but her spine was still straight, her step light, her hair as thick as a girl's, although she had allowed the temples to go gray, giving her an elegant look that could only have benefited from a crown perched thereon. She had a wide smile filled with improbably square teeth, a pug nose, and bright brown button eyes that were naturally inquisitive.

She finished clearing the table and bustled the dishes into the kitchen, leaving him to enjoy the last piece of fry bread and the dregs of his now-lukewarm cocoa in solitary splendor. It was a rectangular room, big enough to hold a table that seated twelve, along with twelve chairs and a sideboard with a hutch on top of it. Flowery prints decorated the walls, which were covered with some tiny floral-print wallpaper in a delicate yellow. There were ruffles on the sheer white curtains hanging at the windows, and tatted tablecloths covered the surface of the table and sideboard and the backs of all twelve chairs. It was a very feminine room, but not so feminine that he felt uncomfortable in it.

He heard the hum of the dishwasher, and shortly Auntie

Vi bustled back in. "Now," she said, sitting down across from him and laying both hands flat against the table. On to business. "What you here for, Jim, eh?"

"Your cocoa and fry bread breakfast."

She shook her head, although she couldn't suppress her smile.

"It would have been worth the flight alone," he said, "but you're right, Auntie, I need your help."

"Ah." She folded her hands and tried to look impassive, but he was not deceived. Auntie Vi loved being asked for help, almost as much as she loved giving it. "With what?"

Her accent was that of a person who spoke English as a second language, a little heavy on the gutturals and a little light on the verbs, but she had no trouble understanding what he was saying. "Good idea," she said when he finished explaining.

"What about office space?"

She shook her head. "Build your own."

"Yeah, I was afraid of that."

"Where you live?"

He met her eyes. "I'd be looking for a small place, probably."

"Uh-huh," she said. "A cabin maybe."

"Maybe," he said.

"Maybe not in village. Maybe down the road a ways."

"Maybe."

He got the hell out of there.

She waited until the door had closed behind him before allowing the wide, all-encompassing grin to spread across her face.

Ayah, that Katya, her life was about to get interesting again. Auntie Vi gave a sharp nod.

Good.

———

Jim went to talk to Billy Mike, implying without actually saying so that Billy Mike was the first person he'd come to. Billy was notoriously easygoing, but he had his pride. Billy's first question was, "You bringing your clerk with you?"

"I hadn't thought," Jim said. "Pretty much up to her. She's pretty dug in in Tok. I don't know that she's going to want to pull the kids out of school. And then there's the housing. I didn't see any FOR SALE signs on my way here."

Billy gave a short, satisfied nod. "Let me know. I'll set you up some interviews."

No doubt he meant with some of his many relatives, but then, the only person who had more relatives in the Park than Billy Mike was Kate Shugak. Jim just hoped that if Billy tossed any of his daughters into the mix that it would be Lilah, who was quick and bright, if a little sharp around the tongue, and not Betsy, who was a major whiner—it was always God or somebody else's fault. Since Lilah was never out of work and Betsy was seldom in, he didn't hold out much hope.

The next thing Billy said was, "You'll have to build."

"I know."

"The Niniltna native association owns a construction company."

"I know."

As he left, Jim reflected that his plans were having unforeseen side effects, which, all told, put him on even more solid footing in the Park than he had been before.

He went to Bobby Clark's next, borrowing Billy's brand-new Ford Explorer (the Eddie Bauer model, this year's Park vehicle of choice at permanent fund dividend time) to get there. The large A-frame on Squaw Candy Creek was set in a densely wooded glen next to a rocky, burbling little creek, the whole frosted with a thick layer of snow so white it was almost blue. It looked like a place you would see from the seat of a sleigh on the way to Grandmother's house, and

Jim paused to admire it before crossing the little bridge and pulling up in front of the deck that extended the width of the house.

Dinah had the door open before he got to the top step, one finger to her lips. He kicked snow from his boots and stepped inside, to see Bobby seated in front of a transmitter, in the middle of a broadcast.

Park Air was not what you could call a scheduled radio show. Nor was it a show licensed or, for that matter, even sanctioned by the Federal Communications Commission. It had a tendency to wander up and down the bandwidth, forcing its listeners to search for it up and down the FM dial. Which would have been easier had Park Air had a fixed schedule and a regular broadcast. It wasn't like Bobby sat down every night at six o'clock to flip switches and send Creedence Clearwater Revival out into the ozone.

And that was another thing: His play list was, well, to put it kindly, somewhat antiquated. Bobby had been born in the fifties and his musical taste had matured in the sixties, and when the seventies came along and brought the Eagles with them, he slammed the door to the tape player in all their faces. Nowadays, when during a broadcast the Park rats heard some John Hiatt, or a little Jimmy Buffett, or sang along to Mary Chapin Carpenter, they knew they had Bobby's wife, Dinah, to thank. Dinah, born in the seventies, now and then liked a little calypso poet in her airtime, and she was not averse to slipping the occasional rogue CD into the pile at Bobby's elbow. Nor was she completely averse to the right bribe.

During the school year, Bobby broadcast advertisements for senior class car washes and junior high bake sales and the school lunch menu for the day, or maybe the week. During an election year, candidates for local and regional offices made the pilgrimage to Bobby's house for an on-air discussion of what the candidate promised to do if he or she was elected, which, since Bobby never believed a word they said and did not hesitate to say so, could get pretty lively. During fishing season, businesses from Cordova, Ahtna, and Valdez advertised nets and impellers and boat hooks.

When someone had a boat, a truck, a band saw, a refrigerator, or a swing set for sale, or needed to buy a crib, a snow machine, a dogsled, or a sled dog, they came to Bobby, paying him with what they had, which was usually fish or game. The result was that Bobby hadn't had to do any of his own hunting since the first year Park Air had gone on the air, and he fished only for the fun of it.

And then there was the Park Post. Bobby was reading from a fistful of scraps of paper, either hand-delivered or mailed to Bobby's post office box in Niniltna. "Bonnie over in Loon Lake, Bonnie over in Loon Lake, Jake in Anchorage says he'll be out this weekend. Hmm. I don't think I'm reading the rest of what he says here, Bonnie, 'cause you might blush. Not to worry, it can be redeemed for a price, small unmarked bills in a plain brown envelope. And the bidding is open!" Bobby crumbled the scrap he was reading from, tossed it over his shoulder, and read the next. "Old Sam Dementieff in Niniltna, Old Sam in Niniltna, Mary Balashoff says for you to get your butt into town for the gun show. 'Gun show,' that's a good one, Mary. Old Sam'll appreciate that." Next scrap. "Mac Devlin in Nabesna, Mac Devlin in Nabesna, your sister Ellen in Omaha just had her first grandchild, a boy, seven pounds, nine ounces, mother Lisa and boy, named Mackenzie for his great-uncle, both doing fine. Congratulations, Mac, and may I proffer a piece of advice? As a much-married and much-fathered man myself, I suggest that you make plans to visit Omaha in about seven years, when little Mackenzie will have acquired at least the veneer of civilization."

A box of Kleenex hit the back of his head and bounced off. Unperturbed, he said, "Also, you won't have to change any diapers."

This time, it was a disposable diaper—clean, fortunately. It bounced down to join the Kleenex.

"Excuse me, folks, I'm getting a little editorial comment from management. Stand by one." He scooped up the diaper, turned in the same movement, and let it sail right back at Dinah. It fell short, but it was a good effort. He went back to the mike. "Christie in Niniltna, Christie in Niniltna, your lawyer wants to talk to you. He says you know the number. Well, that can't be good. My condolences, Christie."

The Park Post was the Park equivalent of jungle drums, putting the father in touch with the fisherman, the fisherman in touch with his banker, the banker in touch with the deadbeat, the deadbeat in touch with the Brown Jug Liquor Store. During cold snaps, when the mercury hit minus double digits and the wind howled down out of the Quilaks, forcing everyone to huddle inside around the woodstove, they turned on the radio to hear Bobby Clark tell them that George was holding their Costco mail order at the hangar until it warmed up enough to hitch the trailer to the snow machine, or that their husband had been weathered in on a caribou hunt ("a likely story," Bobby's invariable comment), or that their daughter had just become engaged, married, or pregnant.

"And last but not least," Bobby said, tossing another crumpled scrap, "Billy and Annie Mike are throwing a potlatch at the school gym this Thursday afternoon in honor of their new son, Cale. Everybody come on by and meet him and have something to eat, and there might even be a dance or two. Okay, time for some music, and none of that wishy-washy, weak-kneed, warbly boy band stuff we got going around today, no sir." Bobby flipped open a case and put a CD in the player. "Here's the Temptations' *Seventeen Greatest Hits* coming at you, except I'm going to skip to the second cut. Why? Because it's my favorite, and because I can! Bye!" He flipped off the mike and punched the play button, and the strains of "My Girl" came out of speakers almost as tall as Jim was, four of them, mounted one to each wall of the room.

"It's enough to make you believe in stereo," Jim said to Dinah.

Bobby wheeled around. "Jim Chopin! As your chopper didn't fill up my show with a bunch of goddamn background noise, I have to assume you were reduced to driving in."

"Yeah, I borrowed Billy's truck."

Bobby's eyes widened. "Holy shit! He let you borrow his new Explorer?" He zipped to the window in his wheelchair, which, given the way he operated it most of the time, seemed like it was jet-propelled. Jim stepped nimbly out of the way of the wheels.

It was easy to remember that Bobby was black—all you had to do was look at him—and, as such, part of a minority measured in the single digits in the Park. It was, however, sometimes hard to remember that he had lost both his legs from the knee on down in a Southeast Asian jungle before he was twenty. His personal history was hazy in between his time in a veteran's rehab clinic and the time he appeared on scene in the Park somewhere around 1978, but whatever he'd been doing in the interim had to have been lucrative, because he'd had enough cash in hand to stake a claim on Squaw Candy Creek, build his A-frame, stock it with enough electronic equipment to keep NASA in business, and buy a vehicle each for air, land, sea, and snow, specially modified, in Bobby's exact phrase, "to get a no-legged gimp anywhere he wants to go in as short a time as possible." He was now the NOAA observer for the Park, calling in weather observations twice a day. Other than that, he seemed to subsist on barter and air, a neat trick, since two years ago Dinah had moved in with him, and a year after that, she presented him with Katya. Dinah, a budding videographer, wasn't pulling in a lot of money herself.

Jim had long ago decided that what Bobby had or had not done before he settled in the Park was none of his business. Bobby drank a lot of Kentucky sipping whiskey, he pirated a little radio wave, and, other than throwing an annual blowout for other Park survivors of the Tet Offensive, lived a quiet life.

And, Jim had enough of the outlaw in himself to recognize another outlaw when he saw one. "Hey, Bobby." He doffed cap and jacket and accepted a mug of steaming coffee from Dinah.

"Goddamn, Chopin!" Bobby said, executing a perfect turn on one wheel with no perceptible traveling. Five point nine, all judges. "How the hell did you talk Billy out of his new wheels?"

Jim moved over to one of the couches surrounding the big rock fireplace set between the ceiling-high windows and sank into very deep cushions. "Well, it's like this."

Bobby and Dinah listened with absorption, and when he was done, they exchanged one of those glances married people give each other, the kind that exchanges a wealth of information without a word being said, and at the same time casts the uncoupled people in the room into outer darkness. "What?" he said.

"Nothing," Dinah said, giving Bobby the look, it being another one of the shorthand methods of married communication.

"No," Bobby said hastily. "Nothing. No wonder Billy gave you his wheels. Anything that brings jobs into the Park makes him happy."

"Even if other people might not be," Dinah said sotto voce, as if she couldn't help herself.

Selective deafness was one of the more useful acquired talents in law enforcement, and Jim practiced it now. "Do you think it'll work?"

Bobby stared at him through narrowed eyes. "Shit. Why ask us—you've already made up your mind."

It wasn't a question, and Jim let a grin be his answer. It was a wide grin, one that could and often did, variously, mesmerize, intimidate, terrify, annihilate, or seduce. Dinah had once heard it described as "the last thing you see before the shark bites" and again as "You know that snake in the movie *The Jungle Book*?" and most recently as "When he's going out the door for the last time, it's like that Judy Garland song, 'The Man That Got Away.' "

As a female female down to her fingertips, Dinah had always been relieved that she had seen Bobby first. Especially since she'd never been one for three-way relationships, and it had been clear from the first time she'd met him that any woman sleeping with Trooper Jim Chopin would be sharing that bed with a third person. It was only recently that she had realized that the third person had never changed, and only in the last year that she had learned to see Jim Chopin as a man instead of a caricature Don Juan. "Hungry?" she said to him. "I was just about to fix us some lunch."

He smiled at her, and she had to repress the instinctive urge to take a step back. Or maybe forward. "Sounds good to me."

They sat down to moose salad sandwiches and ate to the accompaniment of Katya banging her spoon against the tray of her high chair, scattering pureed moose salad all over Bobby's black T-shirt. "Goddamn!" he roared, dabbing ineffectually at his chest. "That's the second shirt today. I thought we was only supposed to be going through diapers by the dozen around here."

"Goddamn!" Katya said, and banged her spoon again.

"Goddamn!" Bobby said, a huge grin on his face. "Did you hear that?"

"Yes," Dinah said.

Bobby saw Dinah's expression and whispered to Katya, "Bad word, honey. Mommy pissed off. We'll talk later."

Katya laughed, a gurgled baby chuckle, and held out her

arms. Her father swooped around the table and scooped her out of her chair, tossing her up in the air. Conversation deteriorated into Park gossip. Had they but known it a re-hash of a similar conversation held not twelve miles down the road the night before, only Bobby had a lot more appreciation to express for Bernie's new barmaid. Dinah gave him a halfhearted swipe and he tucked Katya beneath one arm and scooped Dinah up in the other for a humming, prolonged kiss, which Jim observed with professional approval.

Dinah emerged from the embrace blushing, breathless, and laughing, and Bobby, satisfied, said, "She's a beauty, but cold."

It took Jim a moment to realize that Bobby was talking about the new barmaid. "Oh yeah? What, she said no to you?"

"Cheese it," Bobby hissed, jerking his head at Dinah.

"Sorry."

"I'll say. I don't know, I just don't warm up to her is all. She takes advantage. Dan walked into the Roadhouse the second day after she got there, and as soon as she got his job description, she made a beeline straight for him. Guy didn't have a chance."

"Poor guy," Jim said.

Bobby looked at him and raised an eyebrow.

"Up yours, Clark."

Bobby grinned. "Who else you talking to?"

Jim ticked down a mental list. "You, George, Billy, Auntie Vi. I think I'll head out to Bernie's, see what he says."

"Give my love to the new girl in town," Bobby said, and caught a wet sponge upside the head. "That does it, woman. Now it's war!"

5

An hour after opening time, the Roadhouse was still quiet, and Bernie had time to sit and listen. "Well," he said when Jim came to the end, "it'll sure as hell make my life easier."

"What do you think the general reaction will be?"

Bernie flapped a hand. "Nothing to worry about. Hell, the bootleggers'll run for cover, the dopers will keep their heads low, and ordinary citizens might even think twice about whatever trouble they were planning on getting into. I don't see much but good coming out of it, Jim. And it won't raise my taxes, which always makes me happy."

"Nothing raises your taxes, Bernie; you do business in a federal park."

"Shows how much you know about being an employer," Bernie said. "I just took on a new server—"

"I saw. Yum." He looked around. "Where is she, by the way?"

"She doesn't come on shift until four. She's renting the Gette cabin from the new owners." He looked up from polishing a glass and checked the window. "It's a gorgeous day; she's probably out skiing somewhere. She's a telemarker, she tells me. That's why she moved here—for the snow."

"Oh yeah?"

Bernie leveled a stern forefinger. "You stay away from Christie Turner, goddamn it. She's working out. I don't need her screwed up by some slick talker who only wants to get in her pants."

Jim grinned. Bernie sounded a little wistful, as if sorry he had to follow that rule himself. Edith must be keeping him on a tighter leash than usual. Not that Bernie didn't stray now and then, but strictly when he thought he could get away with it. "I hear she's already taken anyway. Hands off, Scout's honor."

Bernie gave him a skeptical look, but whatever he had been about to say was interrupted by the front door slamming open and banging off the wall.

"Hey!" Bernie said indignantly.

Dandy Mike barreled through the doorway, bundled in down pants and parka, his eyes wide and his expression anxious. He spotted Jim and crossed the floor in hasty steps. "Jim, thank god. You've got to come, right now."

"Where? And why?" Jim stood up. "Dandy. You've got blood all over your pants."

Dandy glanced down, up again. "I know. It's Dina and Ruthe. I went up to deliver their mail, and they're—" He swallowed. "They're dead."

"What?" Bernie said.

"Dina and Ruthe. Somebody broke into their cabin, and Dan—"

"Dan? Dan O'Brian? What about him?"

Dandy swallowed again. "Jim, just come, come right now, okay? Come on."

———

Billy's Explorer made it up the narrow and nearly vertical track to the little cabin, but only just barely, and not without scratching the finish on low-hanging spruce boughs. Dandy's father was going to be pissed.

Dandy pulled his snow machine to a halt in front of the stairs. Jim parked behind him and got out with the briefcase that held his crime-scene kit, without which he never went anywhere. "Hold it, Dandy," he said when Dandy put his foot on the bottom stair. "Let me go first." He checked the camera to see that it held film, got out his notepad and pencil. "Okay," he said, "I don't want you in the room. Stay in the doorway and keep everybody else out."

"Who else?" Dandy said, and even as the words left his mouth, they heard the buzzing of approaching snow machines. He gaped at Jim. "How did you know? How did *they* know?"

"First thing you learn when working out here: The Bush telegraph is faster than the speed of sound. Keep them out."

"Will do," Dandy said, shaken but staunch. Dandy Mike, a charming wastrel with an eye for the ladies every bit as keen as Jim's own, might have a little bit more backbone about him than Jim had previously supposed.

The door, which Dandy had not closed all the way in his haste to depart, slid open with a snick, and Jim stepped inside. He stayed where he was, immobile except for his eyes, which were surveying and cataloging the scene.

His peripheral vision picked up movement, and he crouched and whirled, one hand on his weapon.

It was Dan O'Brian, pulling himself painfully to his feet, looking bloody, bruised, confused, and dazed.

"Dan!" Jim said incredulously. "What the hell?"

And then a second sound made them both jump. One of the bodies on the floor moved, groaned, whimpered. Jim leapt forward, hurdling the piles of pulled-out books and pushing the overturned table in an effort to reach Ruthe

Bauman. Landing next to her, he pressed two fingers against her throat. "Son of a bitch!"

"What's the matter, Jim?" Dandy said from the porch.

"Ruthe's still alive!"

"She can't be!"

"Didn't you check for life signs?"

"I—" Dandy was at a loss. "I didn't even go in after I opened the door. I saw them both lying there covered in blood and Dan standing over them. I thought they were dead. Jesus, Jim, I'm—"

"Never mind that now. Back the truck around!"

He checked Dina's body just to be sure. No pulse, no breath sounds. She was dead, a graceless heap of brittle bone and sagging flesh, her thinning white hair disarranged from its usual neat roll. Her jaw was slack, her mouth a little open. He pulled out his radio, but of course he was out of range. He cursed Dandy for not checking for signs of life more thoroughly, for losing so much precious time in getting Ruthe to help. He cursed himself, too, steadily and out loud, for not bringing the Bell Jet Ranger on this trip.

"Jim?"

"Shut up, Dan."

"Jim, I don't have to say I didn't have anything to do with this."

Jim agonized over whether to move Ruthe, who was on her side, unconscious, colorless, and clammy and who was bleeding from several wounds, including a continuous hor-rific gash across her breasts.

"Jim?"

"Shut up, Dan. Now." There was no blood coming from her mouth or her nose, so he took the chance and rolled her her onto her back to bind her wounds as best he could with dish towels from the kitchen.

"The truck's backed around," Dandy said from the door. He looked like he was going to puke.

"Not in here," Jim said, pointing outside, and Dandy went gladly.

"You'll need something to carry her out on." Dan's voice was steadier, and when Jim looked at him, he seemed back on balance. "Kitchen table?"

It was on its side and one of the legs was broken off. Dan broke off the other three and he and Jim carefully maneuvered a cocooned Ruthe to the top of it. It was a small table, thankfully, but all the same, Jim skinned a knuckle getting it through the door. The stairs were a blasphemous negotiation, but they got the table and Ruthe into the back of the Explorer by putting the backseat down. Jim packed in everything he could find, pillows, bolsters, the cushions from the chairs and couch, anything to keep Ruthe from rolling with the motion of the vehicle. He piled the blankets high and checked her pulse again. Still fast and thready. Her skin hadn't warmed; and she still felt clammy.

"Drive her to Niniltna," Jim said, "and get her on the first plane out of here."

"What?" Dandy said, startled. "You're not taking her in?"

"This didn't happen that long ago, Dandy. I might be able to catch whoever did this."

Dandy looked at the ranger. "Yeah, but Jim—"

Dan looked immensely relieved. Jim didn't have the time, or rather, Ruthe didn't, but he had to ask. "Why are you here?"

"I wanted to ask Dina and Ruthe for help keeping my job," Dan said, nodding at the second snow machine pulled to one side of the yard. "I found them like you saw them. And before you ask, no, I didn't see anyone or hear anything."

"Where'd you get the bruises?"

The ranger looked at Dandy. "I was headed for the door to go for help when this guy barged in." He touched his forehead and winced. "The door caught me in the head and knocked me down. I guess I was out for a while, because next thing I know, you're here."

Jim looked at him. Dan met his eyes without evasion. "What else?"

"Nothing." Dan looked startled. "There isn't anything else."

Time to fish or cut bait. Jim had known Dan O'Brian for fifteen years, and barring the importation of a bottle of blackberry brandy into a dry village for the purposes of stewing up a mess of mallards, the ranger had a crime-free record. He had wanted Dina and Ruthe's help, which eliminated a motive for murder, at least on the face of it. There was no time to waste. Jim made up his mind. "Dan, you ride in the back. Keep her as still as you can."

"What?" Dandy said.

"If she shows blood from the nose or mouth, roll her to one side, but only if she shows the blood."

"Jim—" Dandy said.

Jim turned to Dandy and said, "When you get to the strip, commandeer the first plane out. Get her to Ahtna as fast as you can."

"George was there an—" Dandy looked at his watch "Jesus, was it only fifty minutes ago? He just brought the mail in from Ahtna. That's why I was here—I was bringing them their mail, like I do." Dandy looked down at Ruthe. He might have been about to cry. "It's usually good for a piece of Ruthe's pie."

"Was he turning it around?" At Dandy's blank look, Jim reined in his impatience. "George. Was he turning the plane around for a return trip?"

"I don't know."

"Doesn't matter. Like I said, commandeer the first plane you see and get Ruthe to the hospital in Ahtna. If there isn't a plane there, call the post in Tok. The dispatcher'll know what to do. I'm trying to remember who's on the Niniltna ERT team."

"Uh, the Grosdidier brothers, they live closest to the airstrip."

"Good. Make someone go get 'em if you have to wait for a plane. Don't let her get cold." Jim went to the driver's seat. Billy's new car had come loaded; he turned on the rear heaters full blast. "Get going."

Dandy's panicked expression hardened. "Okay, Jim." He all but saluted and piled in.

"Give her as smooth a ride as possible," Jim said to Dan, closing the door behind him. "I don't know how long those bandages are going to last, and you don't want to jolt them off and have her start bleeding again."

"Okay, Jim," Dan said. He, too, had benefited from the snapped orders. The Explorer's engine turned over and the vehicle inched forward down the track and disappeared almost immediately into the trees.

Jim climbed the stairs to the cabin. It was cold inside, and he pushed the door closed, not without some difficulty, because of the rubble in the way. Everything that had been on a shelf anywhere in the cabin was off it, books, mugs, dishes, pots and pans, cans of food, sacks of flour and sugar and rice, flatware, decks of cards, the top hat token from a Monopoly game, a cribbage board. He took photographs from the door and then picked his way across the debris and took more pictures of Dina's body.

This was the worst part of living where you worked, especially when you worked in law enforcement. Acts of violence were almost always committed against someone you knew, and what was sometimes worse, by someone you knew. He closed his eyes briefly. What if he was wrong? What if Dan O'Brian, contrary to every instinct Jim had, innate or developed on the job, had assaulted the two women? He'd been a practicing police officer for long enough to realize that anyone can kill, given the right motivation.

Dina had been a crusty old broad with a salty tongue, a

ribald sense of humor, and a fount of stories that reflected no good on anyone elected or appointed to public office since Alaska had become a state. Jim had spent more than a few hours sitting at a Roadhouse table with Dina Willner, listening to those tales, tales that went all the way back to the first days of Camp Teddy, and even further back to her days as a WASP in World War II, first in Texas and then in Florida. She had forgotten more about flying than he would ever learn, and she was willing to share. He had liked her. He had liked her a lot, and now someone had killed her. It made him angry, the way murder always made him angry. There, he thought, there was motivation for you.

He righted the couch and placed Dina's body on it. Her limbs were loose—rigor had not set in—which meant that the killer was not long gone. He thought of Dan, jolting down the hill in the back of the Explorer. He found in a heap behind the couch a homemade quilt that looked like something the four aunties would make. He spread it over her, then stood silently before her for a few moments.

A draft of cold air made him shiver, and he looked around, noticing for the first time that the back door was open, too. He unbuckled the flap of his holster and stepped to it. Unlike the front door, this one was solid wood, no window, no line of sight. He pushed it open cautiously with his left hand, his weapon drawn and held next to his thigh. The bottom of the door scraped over packed-down snow. There was no movement beyond it. He stepped out on the porch.

It was smaller than the front porch and shadowed by the overhanging trees. A narrow path led through them and up the precipitous slope to the outhouse, a neat wooden structure painted brown, with only the bottom half of a door. Jim thought that was odd until he climbed up and saw the view, which began at the cabin's ridgepole and continued on, if you had the imagination for it, all the way to Prince William Sound.

He looked down at the cabin and saw what he'd missed when he had stepped outside: an overturned plate, with what looked like some kind of stew spilled next to it. He slid back down and looked. Yes, stew—meat, some carrots, potatoes, celery, and onions in a thick gravy. He touched it. It was frosting over, but it wasn't quite frozen.

Were Dina and Ruthe in the habit of eating their lunch on the back porch? He thought it unlikely, especially in midwinter, but if he was wrong, why only one plate? And what had caused the spill? Had Ruthe or Dina been outside eating as the assailant entered through the front door? Had the beginning of the attack startled whoever was on the back porch into dropping the plate and then walking in on the scene?

Unsatisfied, he turned around and surveyed the hillside again. There was the trail to the outhouse, trodden down so that the surface was hard, with more snow piled waist-high on either side. There weren't any other tracks, except—wait a minute. He went up the trail again, this time at a trot, and discovered that the trail continued on behind the outhouse and farther up the hill. This trail was not so well packed down, showing separate footprints marking a far less frequent passage.

He was a big man with long legs. The snow was very deep and the hill very steep. His progress was slow. Once, the trail narrowed in, so that it seemed as if he wouldn't be able to squeeze through the trees.

It was a glorious afternoon. The trees were thick with frost, ghosts of their original selves. The sky was clear and cold and the dull blue, off-white of a glacier's face with the sun on it. The sun itself was a flat flaxen disk, low on the horizon, leached of light and warmth.

Fighting the spruce all the way, he emerged finally, out of breath and soaked in his own sweat, on a miniature plateau. On this plateau, the trees had been thinned out to make way for a scattering of tiny cabins, all with snow up to their eaves. From one of the chimneys, a spiral of smoke whispered up into the clear blue sky. The trail led directly to it.

He unholstered his weapon again when he was ten feet from the door. He didn't see how whoever lived there could not have heard him coming, given the water buffalo nature of his approach, but he made himself wait and listen for signs of life.

There was a lot of yellow snow around the door, as if the resident couldn't be bothered to break a trail to the outhouse. He peered into the window cut into the wall next to it. It was covered with a blanket of some kind. He looked in the window on the other side of the door. Same thing.

The door opened out, naturally. He would have traded warm feet for the portable ram in his Cruiser back in Tok.

He paused for a moment of procedural reflection. Was he in hot pursuit? Did he have to knock and identify, or not? More importantly, if he knocked, was whoever lived there standing on the other side with a shotgun?

Snow was collecting inside the tops of his boots and the sweat was freezing on his spine. The hell with it. He thumped on the door. "Hello? Anybody home? This is Alaska state trooper Jim Chopin. Open the door, please."

There was no reply, and no movement from within.

The silence of an Arctic winter day in the Bush, when no breeze stirred the air and the sun beat down coldly over all, that was a silence to be reckoned with. It was a silence with unfriendly eyes that glared out at you for disturbing it. When a magpie yelled at him from a nearby tree, he nearly jumped out of his skin. Annoyed, he thumped on the door again. "Police! Open up!"

There was loud, wild *Wraaaaaooooowl* right next to his head. He jumped back to the edge of the porch and slipped off the top step. His arms windmilled wildly and he fell heavily on his back. "Son of a bitch!"

There was another inhuman howl, and a black house cat

jumped down from a timber just below the roof of the porch. Her hair standing straight out from her body, she looked like a big black porcupine. Her eyes were wild and her fur was stained red. She hit the porch once, bounced off it and landed on his chest, leaving red paw prints on his dark blue jacket, bounced off again and landed on the trail, skimming over the snow as if it wasn't there and vanishing into the trees at a dead run.

"Oh shit," he said, remembering Dina and Ruthe's cat for the first time. They had called her Galadriel, after Ruthe's favorite wood witch, and over the years the name had naturally been shortened to Gal. She was a longtime member of the family and, what was even more important, a legendary greeter of Camp Teddy's summer guests. Gal had purred from the laps of the rich and powerful for a decade. If Ruthe survived, Gal would be the first person Ruthe would want to see. He wallowed around until he managed to get to his feet. "Gal! Here, kitty! Come on, Gal, you know me! Come on back now!"

From inside the cabin came a faint sound—a whimper, perhaps a moan? He whipped around, discovered his hand was empty, and had to go rooting for his weapon. He found it, then had to clear the muzzle and the trigger guard of snow. He hoped the damn thing didn't explode in his hand if he had to fire it.

What was that sound he had heard? Perhaps nothing at all? Jim climbed to the porch again and tried the handle of the door. The latch gave.

"Hello the house. This is Alaska state trooper Jim Chopin. I'm coming inside." The door swung open, creaking.

The sound came again, definitely a whimper this time. He brought his weapon up two-handed and pointed it inside before entering. "This is state trooper Jim Chopin. Who's in here?"

There was another whimper, and then his eyes adjusted from the blazing sun of the exterior to the murky darkness of the interior of the cabin. It was tiny, ten feet to a side, with twin beds pushed against two walls, a small table and a captain's chair set against a third. A small cast-iron wood-stove stood in one corner next to a nearly empty wood box. Scrolled wooden shelves were fixed to two walls, and there were three windows, all of them iced over on the inside. To the right of the door was a counter with a two-burner pro-pane hot plate, a tin bowl, and a plastic jug half-full of what looked like water. There was a kettle on the hot plate. A box of Lipton's tea bags, a container of dried lemon peel, and a jar of honey sat on the counter. On the wall above was a propane lamp.

One of the beds was neatly made, the other heaped with an olive drab duffel bag stenciled US ARMY in black Marks-A-Lot, white T-shirts, a couple of plaid men's shirts, a pair of jeans, shorts, and a few pair of thick wool socks, which looked uncomfortably like the ones on the body of the woman in the cabin down the hill. Everything was neatly folded and laid out with almost geometrical precision in relation to everything else.

The stove was giving off very little heat, which was prob-ably why the man was crouched down next to it, wedged against the wall between the stove and the table, and why Jim almost missed him. He was a little man, very thin, and Jim would have mistaken him for a heap of clothes had the man not whimpered again.

His hair was dirty blond going gray and hadn't been washed or cut in a while. His eyes peered out from behind it, feral, shifty, shy, not meeting Jim's. He whimpered again.

"Sir," Jim said, lowering his weapon. "I'm Alaska state trooper Jim Chopin, and . . ."

His voice faded out as he took a step forward. The front of the man's clothing was covered in a dark substance that looked like dried blood.

So was the knife he held.

Without realizing it, Jim raised his gun. "All right, sir, could you put the knife down, please?"

Another whimper. "Sir, put the knife down. Now."

The man pushed himself into his corner, drawing up his knees and hiding behind his arms. He mumbled something.

"What? Sir, I couldn't hear you. What did you say?"

Dazed eyes blinked up at him. He mumbled something else.

It sounded like "angels," "angels" and something else. Jim swore to himself. He didn't want to put himself within striking range of someone who was seeing angelic apparitions, but there didn't seem to be a lot of choice, other than shooting the man outright. He transferred the Smith & Wesson nine-millimeter automatic to his left hand and took a step forward. "I'm going to take the knife, sir, all right? That's it, just relax. No one's going to hurt you. That's right, just hand it over. Let's everybody stay calm and no one will get hurt."

He continued with a steady stream of soothing babble as he inched forward, making no sudden movements as he bent his knees and reached out with his right hand, hoping he wasn't reaching out with it for the last time. "That's right, sir, just keep calm, keep still—"

The man pushed against the floor with his feet in a sudden movement that added ten years to Jim's life. "Sir. Sir. Please stay still. You might cut yourself, and we don't want that, do we?" He continued to move forward and the man continued to cringe away, his face buried in his arms, the knife clenched in his left fist. Jim's hand was two feet away, one foot, six inches. "That's it, sir, stay very still."

He took hold of the knife at the part of the handle protruding above the man's hand. More whimpering, more cringing, but to Jim's infinite relief, the man's grip relaxed and the knife slid free.

Jim took a deep breath. He took several. "Okay. That's

good." He backed away and stood up. He always kept a couple of gallon-size Ziplocs in his inside pocket, and he placed the knife in one of them. He wrapped a second bag around the first and stored the bundle in a pocket. "Sir? Sir? Could you stand up? Come on, sir, I won't hurt you." He took a chance and holstered his weapon. "Come on. Stand up now."

He pulled the man to his feet. The man came up without resistance. His hair fell back and Jim saw that his face was stained with tears. "Did you hurt the cat?" the man said.

"No, sir," Jim said, surprised at the intelligible sentence. "She's down at the main house by now." He devoutly hoped he was telling the truth. "Sir, what is your name?"

The man stared at him. "What?"

"What is your name? Who are you? What are you doing in this cabin?"

The man looked around him, a sudden wide smile that was as bright as it was meaningless spreading across his face. "Isn't this a nice place? The nicest I ever stayed in." He shivered. "Cold, though."

He was older than Jim had first thought. His face was lined and his beard and hair were an untrimmed tangle of curls that fell to his shoulders and chest. He looked like a cross between a mad scientist and the Count of Monte Cristo before the escape. He smelled of wood smoke and urine. Jim looked down and saw that the man had wet his pants.

"You shouldn't entertain angels unawares," the man said suddenly.

Jim looked at him askance. The man flashed his mad smile again. "You know why?"

"No," Jim said. "Why?"

The man's voice dropped to a confiding level. "Because they can turn out to be the devil."

Come to think of it, the guy looked more like Rasputin

than the Count. "Okay, sir, let's go back down to the lodge."

The man cringed and tried to pull free. "No! No, I don't want to go there! The devil's there!"

"Not anymore," Jim said.

On the way back, all he could think of was how relieved he was that Dan O'Brian was off the hook.

And how not wrong he had been to let him go with Ruthe.

6

The news of the attack on Dina Willner and Ruthe Bauman and of Dina's death swept around the Park faster
than if it had been broadcast on Park Air. The news
that Trooper Jim Chopin had a suspect in custody swiftly
succeeded it.

Kate heard it from Johnny, who came home from town
with the news the following afternoon. She sat down hard
and stared at nothing for several long moments. Johnny
shifted from foot to foot, uneasy at the vacant expression
on her face. "Kate?" he said tentatively. "Are you all right?"

She said nothing.

"Kate," he said, and stepped forward to touch her on the
shoulder.

She looked at him. "What?"

"Are you all right?"

Two of her grandmother's oldest friends had just been
butchered, one of them to death, the other to near death.
"Yes," she said, summoning up a smile from who knew
where. "I'm all right, Johnny."

He watched her indecisively for a moment. "Want some cocoa?"

"What? No, I don't think so."

" 'Cause I was going to make some for myself."

She saw from the look on his face that he needed something to do. "I'll take some tea. Some Lemon Zinger, with honey."

He brightened. "Great. I can do that." He went to the woodstove and checked the kettle, which was always left to steam gently at the back. "Almost full," he said. He got out two mugs, measured Nestlé's and evaporated milk into one and honey into another. He put the tag of the tea bag underneath the bottom of the mug with honey in it. "So when you pour the water in, the string and tag don't go in, too," he said. He looked over his shoulder. Kate was back to staring into space.

It was the first time Johnny had had to carry news of the dead and dying to anyone, and the task made him feel very odd. He wondered if Kate had felt like this when she had come to tell him his father had been killed. For the first time, he wondered how she had managed. She'd almost been killed, too, or so they said, because she had never mentioned it. She'd been moving slowly and carefully that day, he remembered, as if it hurt to do normal stuff like walk and sit. She'd had bandages on her arm, her hands and face had been skinned and bruised, and the hair that used to hang to her waist in a big fat black braid had been sheared off, all raggedy, not even and neat like it was now. He wondered who had cut it off, and why. He wondered why she didn't let it grow back.

He knew Ruthe and Dina, too, maybe not as well as Kate, but well enough. He'd been to their cabin several times since he'd moved to the Park, and he'd liked the two ladies, even if they were older than God. Dina had started right in on him, wanting to know how much he knew about the Park and what lived in it. He was interested, and she didn't talk down to him, so he didn't mind. She had showed him a photo album that started out with weird little rectangular black-and-white pictures and ended up with normal ones—in color, with digital date stamps in the corners. There were pictures of bears and moose, and one of two bald eagles fighting each other in the air, only Dina had said they were mating. There was a picture of Dina standing twenty feet in front of a walrus haul, with what must have been thousands of walrus, and a picture of Ruthe standing in what looked like the middle of a vast herd of caribou, the animals stretching out all around her, over an immense plain, as far as the eye could see. A mink peeked out of a snowbank; a beaver got caught slapping his tail; a wolverine, fangs bared, looked like he was about to charge. "He was, too," Dina had said, cackling; "we barely got out of there in time."

There were pictures of tracks of every kind—in the mud of spring and the swamp of summer, but mostly in the snow: the long stride and enormous feet of a wolf, the smaller prints of a fox, and the tiny prints of a vole.

In one picture, the hip-hopping tracks of an arctic hare vanished, just stopped altogether. "See?" Dina had said, pointing. Feathered ends of wing tips left a ghostly clue in the show on either side of the tracks.

"Wow," Johnny had said, awed.

"A golden eagle, from the wingspan. *Aquila chrysaetos,*" Dina had said, and she had made him repeat the words until he had the pronunciation correct. "Of the family Accipitridae."

"I've only ever seen bald eagles," he had said humbly, and when she'd turned the page, there was a picture of a golden eagle in flight, at about five hundred feet up, the photo shot from the window of a plane. He could see part of one strut.

"Is that a Super Cub?" he said.

Dina was impressed. "Yes."

"Is it yours?"

She nodded. "It's at the strip in Niniltna. How did you know it was a Cub?"

He looked back at the picture of the golden eagle. "My dad was a pilot."

"I know. I met him. He drove a Cessna, didn't he?"

"Yeah. A one seventy-two."

"I remember. Lycoming conversion."

"Yeah."

"Sweet little plane. What happened to it?"

"My mom sold it when my dad died."

The kitchen timer had dinged then and Ruthe had taken a sheet of cookies out of the oven, the best oatmeal cookies he'd ever eaten. She sent him home with a bagful. She was pretty, and as smart as Dina. He'd liked them both, and he was sorry there would be no more evenings spent at their cabin eating fresh-baked goodies out of the oven and looking at pictures of otters sliding down a snowbank into a creek.

The tea had steeped and melted the honey and he'd stirred all the lumps out of the cocoa. He added marshmallows to the cocoa and carried both mugs to the table, sitting down across from her. "How long did you know them?"

"Hmm? What?" She looked down and saw the mug. "Oh. Thanks." She curved her hands around it, warming her fingers, which felt suddenly cold.

"So how long did you know them?"

"Ruthe and Dina?" She stared down at the surface of the tea, a golden yellow. "All my life. They were friends of my grandmother."

He nodded, very serious, and wiped marshmallow from his mouth. "Emaa."

"Yes."

"And she's dead, too."

"Yes."

"Is the tea all right?"

"What? Oh." She sipped at the tea for form's sake. "Yes, it's fine. Thanks, Johnny."

"You're welcome."

She put up a hand to rub her forehead. "It's hard to believe. They seemed, I don't know, larger than life. Like they'd live forever."

"Like Dad," Johnny said, nodding.

She looked at him then. "What?"

"Like Dad," Johnny repeated. She didn't think he knew it when a tear slid down his cheek. "He was like, I don't know, God. I didn't think anything could hurt him. Well, except you."

He was only fourteen and he'd been orphaned by one parent and had orphaned himself from the second as a deliberate act. He was trying so hard to act grown-up, to take matters like divorce and separation and death in his stride, to be independent and autonomous and to move on and keep moving without looking back. Kate knew the feeling.

She didn't make the mistake of denying she'd ever hurt his father, and she didn't try to apologize. "I know. He was kind of . . . indestructible, I guess."

"Except when he died," Johnny said.

"Except when he died," Kate said.

"Can you tell me now?" Johnny said in a low voice. "Can you tell me what happened?"

"I told you what happened, Johnny. Those hunters we were guiding started shooting at each other, and we got in the way."

"All of it, this time," Johnny said.

She met the blue eyes fixed so determinedly on her face, saw the pleading look in them. His whole body was tensed with the need to know of his father's last hours on earth. It wasn't that she hadn't meant to tell him the whole story one day, when he was older and could handle it. And she could handle telling it.

"Can you? Please, Kate?"

It seemed, after all, that she could.

She followed Johnny into town the next morning, waving good-bye as he took the turn for the school gym, where Billy was having his new baby party. Johnny wanted to learn to dance, and Park Air had announced there might be dancing. Besides, he liked Billy, and he thought it was cool that he had a new baby all the way from Korea. He'd looked up Korea on Kate's atlas, so he felt ready.

Kate's first stop was the Step. She walked into Dan's office, Mutt at her heels, to find the ranger with his feet propped on the sill of the window and his hands laced behind his head. He had a moody expression on his face. "Hey," she said.

He dropped his feet but not his hands, until Mutt insisted on a head scratch. "Hey."

Kate sat down opposite him. "I heard."

"I figured."

"You okay?"

"I been suspended."

"What?"

He tossed her a sheet of paper with the National Park Service letterhead; it was addressed to the chief ranger and placed him on suspension indefinitely, pending the outcome of the criminal investigation into the death of Dina Willner. Kate looked up. "I thought Jim had a suspect in custody."

"He does."

"Then what's this crap?"

"Any stick'll do to beat a dog with, Kate." He looked at Mutt. "Sorry, babe. They want to get rid of me. It's probably enough that I stumbled into the middle of a murder. Guilt by association."

Kate tossed the paper into the garbage can. "You're not going to put up with this shit, are you?"

"Well," Dan said, shifting his gaze from the window to Kate, "there's not a whole hell of a lot I can do about it. Of course, I'm the only one on duty at this time of year, and it'll take a while before they find someone qualified to take over. I doubt that any of the suits in Anchorage are going to want to leave the bright lights and the big city to baby-sit in the wilderness."

"Dan."

"Kate—"

"You may be going to put up with this, but I'm not."

He drew a deep breath and expelled it slowly. "I went there to ask Dina and Ruthe for their help in keeping this job. You got me so fired up last time we talked that I figured you were right, that I ought to fight for it, not just sit back and let my friends carry the weight. But now I don't know. Dina's *dead*, Kate, and Ruthe might die. Two great old broads, one gone, one maybe gone. Nothing else seems all that important right now."

Kate leaned forward. "Dina and Ruthe would be the first to tell you that the land is what's important, Dan. Not us. The land. We're only custodians, and temporary ones at that. We do the best we can and then we pass the job along to the next generation. I don't think you're ready to hand off just yet."

He looked at her with the faint glimmer of his old smile. "You be careful there, Shugak. You're starting to sound like your grandmother."

She sat back. "Did you see the guy Jim brought in?"

He shook his head.

"Did you see anything yourself?"

"No." He seemed about to say something else, then repeated firmly, "No. I didn't see anything. It doesn't matter, really, if I saw anything or didn't see anything. Jim got the guy. Crazy bastard, sounds like," he added as an afterthought.

It sounded like the truth, she thought as she made her

way back down the trail from the Step. It also sounded like Dan was trying to convince himself that it was. Which was crazy. Like Dan said, Jim got the guy, had him in custody in Ahtna. Case closed.

The sky had clouded over in the night and the temperature had warmed up to ten above, and if the rising barometer at the homestead was working right, there was a storm coming in off the Gulf. She drove through Niniltna to the turnoff and then, for the second time that week, negotiated the narrow track to the little cabin perched high on the side of the mountain. The snow in the yard was packed down hard from the passage of many vehicles, wheeled and tracked, and there were a couple of snow machines already parked there. She stopped hers and climbed the stairs.

There were two strange men in the house, men she'd never seen before. They swung around, startled, when the door opened. "Who the hell are you, and what are you doing here?" she said.

They were both in their early twenties, hairy and with the aroma of an unwashed winter about them. They hadn't bothered to doff their Carhartt jackets, bib overalls or their knit caps, only their identical pairs of black leather gloves. "Just poking around," one of them said. "Seeing if there's something we can use."

Both of them were looking at Mutt, who was standing at Kate's side and looking both of them over with a long, considering stare. Mutt was half wolf, and when she wanted to, she let it show. Sensing Kate's rising anger, she bared a little fang.

The man who had spoken visibly paled. "Look, we're not doing anything wrong. The two old ladies are dead, they don't have any relatives, and—"

"Wrong," Kate said flatly. "I'm their relative. Get out."

He tried to bluster. "Who the hell are you anyway? You'll just take all the good stuff if—"

"Russ," the other man said.

"Well, hell, Gabe, we got here first. We're not going to turn around and—"

"That's Kate Shugak."

"What?"

The other man nodded at Kate. "That's Kate Shugak."

"Oh." Russ gulped. "And that must be—"

"Mutt."

Mutt had perfected the art of the unblinking stare. It could be unnerving.

"Oh." Russ gulped again. "Actually, we were just leaving."

"That we were," the second man said, and beat him out the door.

Mutt looked up at Kate and raised an eyebrow. Kate shook her head. "Not worth it." Mutt gave an almost-perceptible shrug. "Find Gal," Kate said. Mutt looked disgusted and stalked out, disapproval evident in the slightly backward set of her ears.

The room looked as if it had been hit by a chinook, one of the spring storms that roared up out of the Gulf like a lion and proceeded to blow everything in front of it out of the way. There wasn't really any good place to start. Kate shed parka, bib, and boots and rolled up her sleeves. Finding that someone had banked the embers in the woodstove, she loaded it with wood, and waded in.

The bookshelves were freestanding and had been pulled down, but they'd been emptied of books and so were easy enough to stand back up. She began putting books in at random, figuring they could be organized later. She righted furniture, replaced the canned goods and pots, pans, and dishes—plastic, a good thing—in the cupboards, and cleaned up those supplies that had been spilled, mostly flour—both wheat and white, it looked like. Most of a forty-eight-ounce bag of chocolate chips was spilled across the floor, too. She swept it all up and into a garbage bag, which she tied off and put on the porch. The bears were asleep, and she'd get the bag to the dump before they woke up again in the spring.

A lone bunny slipper, one of its ears lopsided, was sitting on its side under the woodstove. Kate fished it out and put it on a shelf, unable to stop the tears from welling in her eyes. She conducted a search but couldn't find the other one. Maybe it was with Dina's body.

There didn't seem to be a dish towel to be found, or a towel of any kind, and then she remembered. Ruthe had been hurt, and transported to the hospital. Someone had probably used them for bandages. She climbed the ladder to the loft and discovered, somewhat to her surprise, that the chinook had hit here, as well. The two beds were off their stands, a pillow leaked feathers, and clothes had been emptied from closets and drawers and were strewn all over the floor. The blankets were gone. Ruthe again, she figured. She got the beds back on their stands, the clothes back into place, and as much of the leaky pillow and its errant feathers as possible into another garbage bag.

When Ruthe got better, Kate didn't want her coming home to a destroyed house. If she didn't get better . . . No, she would.

She went to the top of the ladder and turned around, hands on the posts, foot on the first rung, and gave the loft a long look. Pale light leaked in from a skylight in the ceiling.

Why the loft? The two women had been assaulted downstairs. Why beat up on two women and then trash the loft? Seemed like overkill. She winced at the word. Dan had called the perp a "crazy bastard." That could be all it was. Enough crazy bastards came into the Park and misbehaved that it was usually enough of an explanation, requiring the full-time attention of three troopers and more than a few tribal policemen. Hell, there were enough of the home-grown variety to keep everyone in business, never mind the newbies.

She climbed down the ladder and began to try to make sense of some of the letters and paperwork that she had piled on the coffee table. There were advisory reports on this and that species of wildlife, letters asking for endorsements in political campaigns and for a presence at fundraisers, some from candidates whose names made Kate's eyebrows go up. There were fat files on various parks and refuges, environmental-impact studies on a couple of construction projects, including a hiking trail someone wanted to run down the side of the Kanuyaq River from Ahtna all the way to Cordova; it would run partway along the existing roadbed into the Park.

She noticed for the first time that Ruthe and Dina had no family photographs, no pictures of mothers, fathers, grandparents, brothers or sisters. She shrugged. Maybe they were both orphans. Still, it seemed odd. Everybody had pictures of people, at least a few. Ruthe and Dina's albums were of plants, animals, glaciers, avalanches, and mountaintops, and if there were people in them, they were usually Ruthe or Dina.

Then she found one with both of them and Ekaterina, posing in front of the Kanuyaq Copper Mine, along with a crowd of other people. The beaver-hatted man on Emaa's right must be Mudhole Smith, the Bush pilot from Cordova. All four aunties were there, three with their husbands, who were still living at the time. Demetri Totemoff and John Letourneau were standing shoulder-to-shoulder, which would put the date back in the days before they'd split their guiding business and gone their separate ways. John was standing next to Dina and laughing down at her. Anastasia was next to Demetri, looking up at him with a soft smile. Demetri's arm was draped tentatively around her, as if he had yet to be convinced that he had the right. He probably still feared the appearance of Anastasia's father with a gun, which, from everything Kate had heard, would have been just like Frank Korsakovakof. A protective father and a good man. Anastasia had found it hard to go up against him, so the story went, but Demetri had prevailed, and in the end, Frank had come around. And now both Frank and Anastasia were gone. She made a mental note to stop in and see Demetri soon.

In the photograph, the polyester clothes and the hair, either board-straight or permed to a curlicue, put the time in the mid- to late seventies. They all looked tanned and fit, and so very vigorous. So alive. There was a man standing to the right and a little behind Ekaterina. Kate took a closer look. Ray Chevak, from Bering. Emaa's—what? Even back then, he wasn't young enough to be called "boyfriend."

It was unnerving to see how far back Ray and Ekaterina's relationship went. Kate hadn't known about it until after Emaa's death, and she didn't want to know more, didn't want her imagination to work out any of the details.

She heard a noise on the porch and went to the door. Mutt was on the top step, Gal between her front paws, her face screwed up into an expression of deep distaste as Mutt washed her with a raspy pink tongue. They both became aware of Kate at the same moment. Gal sprang away and hissed. *Grr,* Mutt said in return. Gal jerked her tail and padded between Kate's legs. She gave an imperious meow, but when Kate got her some food, she barely waved a whisker over it before going right to Ruthe's chair and curling up.

"Welcome home," Kate said. She was immensely relieved. She didn't want to have to tell Ruthe that Gal had disappeared. She bent to give the cat a scratch behind the ears and found her fur damp to the touch from Mutt's ministrations. She looked over at Mutt. "You make a pretty good nurse."

Mutt gave an elaborate yawn, and cleaned up Gal's food with a single swipe of her tongue. It was all show, because Kate knew for a fact that Mutt had dined very nicely the day before on the remains of a moose carcass not a mile from the homestead.

She noticed a book she had missed beneath the sofa and bent down to pick it up. Wedged under the couch was a narrow tin box, of the size to hold standard file folders. It was locked. Kate looked for a key in hopes that there might be names and numbers for her to call—not that either Dina or Ruthe had ever referred to having anyone to call in the event of, other than each other. There was a key rack with hooks sprouting from little tin chickadees, with airplane keys, snow machine keys, and truck keys, but no keys to fit the tin box. She set the box to one side, not feeling things were to the point that she had to break into it.

"Hey," a voice said from the deck.

She looked up, to behold Jim Chopin peering at her through the window. She didn't notice that the sight of him didn't cause its usual knee-jerk antipathy. "Hey, yourself."

He came in. "What are you doing here?"

She waved a hand. "Trying to clean up for when Ruthe gets home."

He looked at her and forbore from saying what was on both their minds.

"You?" she said.

He shrugged. "I don't know. I think I wanted to see if I'd remembered to lock the door."

"There's no lock."

He examined the doorknob. "I'll be damned."

"Dina didn't believe in locks in the Bush. Said if she and Ruthe were both away from home and somebody got lost in a blizzard that she wanted them to be able to get in."

"I don't know who'd stagger up this mountain in a blizzard, but it's a nice thought."

"I caught a couple of guys poking through the rubble."

His eyes sharpened. "Who?"

She shook her head. "Don't know them. I ran them off."

"Get tags?"

She shook her head again. "I don't think they'll be back. And I'll get Bernie to spread the word that I'm looking after the place."

Which all by itself would be enough to keep the cabin and the surrounding property sacrosanct, Jim thought. At least for a while, at least until they knew if Ruthe would live.

"I hear you got the guy," she said.

"Yeah. Knife in hand. Blood wasn't even dry on it. Tests already confirmed Ruthe's and Dina's blood on it."

"That was quick."

"The governor himself called the crime lab. Love them or hate them, Ruthe and Dina helped make a lot of the history of this state. He ordered the flags to fly at half-staff today."

In spite of herself, Kate was impressed. "A nice gesture."

"Yeah, ought to pick him up a few more votes in the next election." Gal's head poked up over the back of the chair, and Jim said, "Hey, Gal, you came back! Good girl. Thank god. I couldn't find her after she took off."

He told Kate what had happened, and she laughed, surprising both of them. He picked up Gal and sat down with her in his lap, where she immediately curled up, purring and kneading. Mutt padded over and rested her chin on the arm of the chair, and Jim freed a hand to scratch her ears.

Kate sat down and started going through the paperwork again. When next she looked up, Jim had his head against the back of the chair and his eyes closed. Gal was curled into a soft black ball on his lap and Mutt was stretched out on the floor with her head on one of his feet.

It was quite a domestic scene. Kate went back to the paperwork, but her mind was more on the man across from her.

They called him "Chopper Jim" because of his preferred method of transportation, a Bell Jet Ranger helicopter, although he flew fixed-wing, too, and was reliable and skilled on both craft.

They also called him "the Father of the Park," for his equally reliable and skilled seduction of pretty much every available female inside Park boundaries. Although now that Kate thought of it, she couldn't remember any children whose mothers claimed he had fathered them. A courtesy title, perhaps, and Kate was a little startled when the thought made her smile.

He was originally from California, which figured. He had the same coloring as Ethan, only darker, and he was tall, also like Ethan, but he was much broader in the beam. He looked like a buff Beach Boy, and she'd bet he had spent his entire childhood in the water with a surfboard. What was he doing in Alaska, three thousand miles and one time zone away, with no sand, no surf, and no beach bunnies? It was a question she'd never asked him.

He'd stuck. He'd been posted to the Park the year before she graduated from the University of Alaska at Fairbanks, and they had howdied when she spent her vacations in the Park, but they hadn't really shook until she had quit working as an investigator for the Anchorage district attorney and had come home with attitude to spare and a scar that stretched across her throat almost from ear to ear. Unlike many of the Park rats, he hadn't treated her as fragile, about to break. Instead, he'd made a move, she had rebuffed it, and that had set the pattern of their relationship—she couldn't call it friendship, not even after Bering—from then until now.

As a trooper, he had what she thought was a real understanding of the difference between the letter and the spirit of the law, and sometimes, she had to admit, the almost-inspired ability to enforce one without violating the other. That business with Cindy and Ben Bingley two breakups before. And Johnny this fall, when he had sided with the boy—and her—against the boy's mother and legal guardian, in essence aiding and abetting what could be construed in a court of law as kidnapping.

Emaa had approved of him, in her austere fashion. That alone was enough to guarantee Kate's antagonism. For the first time, Kate wondered if it had been deliberate. Emaa had been a master manipulator, and while she was alive, Kate had fought a constant rear-guard action to keep her grandmother from taking over her life. Emaa had liked Jack, too. Although Kate had brought Jack home as a fait accompli, already a fixture in her life, and Emaa would have found acceptance more expedient than antagonism. Emaa had been the compleat political animal, even in her relationships with family members. A smile curled the corners of Kate's mouth, and her eyes strayed again to the man sleeping across the table from her.

Not that she would have felt differently about Jim if Emaa had not approved of him. She finished neatening up the paperwork and stacked it in a pile, dividing it by year with file folder separators. The pile was tall enough to teeter. She moved it to a corner, where she leaned it up against a wall and weighted it down with a frayed tome four inches thick, *Harper's Dictionary of Classical Literature and Antiquities*. What on earth had the old girls needed with that?

The stove was burning low and she added a couple of logs before going to the kitchen and setting the kettle to boil. She was hungry, and with a glance over her shoulder, she pulled out a couple of cans of cream of tomato soup and a package of saltines. There was butter in the cooler outside, miraculously spared by the attacker, or perhaps just overlooked.

Jim stirred when she set the tray down on the coffee table. "Hey," he said, yawning. "Guess I fell asleep."

"Yeah," she said. "Soup's on."

"Be right back." He gently assisted Gal from his lap and stepped outside. Mutt, with similar intentions, and finding herself on the wrong side of the door, barked once. The door opened and she slipped out.

"Mutt's causing havoc with the local wildlife," Jim said when he came back in. "I saw her flush out a couple of spruce hens. Good thing the girls aren't here to see."

"What a phony. She's not that hungry; she chowed down on the better part of a moose yesterday."

"Dogs just wanna have fun."

"That dog does. Have some soup and crackers."

"Thanks."

They ate in silence. "Thanks," he said again when he was finished, sitting back and combing his hair back with one hand. "Sorry I fell asleep. I didn't think I was that tired."

"You up all night with the perp?"

"Higgins? Pretty much."

"That's his name?"

"Riley K. Higgins, that's him."

"What set him off?"

"He's not talking." He buttered another cracker. "He's pretty pitiful, really. We got a make on his prints. He's a vet, two tours in Vietnam, never really got back to the world. Came from Carbondale, Illinois, originally. His dad's dead. I talked a little to his mom."

"How was she?"

He bit into the cracker and chewed meditatively. "Like her son died in Vietnam and she's been mourning his loss ever since. She sounds frail. I didn't talk to her long. I called the local police chief. He said Higgins was on the street, got picked up for pretty much everything at one time or another—indecent exposure for peeing in an alley, drunk in public, disturbing the peace. Got beat up once, bad enough to be in the hospital and dry out. Didn't take. He also got run in for drugs a time or two, but only marijuana, nothing serious. Nothing expensive anyway. Nothing violent, either, which bothers me some. Usually there's a pattern you can trace back when something like this happens.

"The chief said he disappeared last summer. Said the family's a good bunch and that they had done everything they could for him, but he thinks that by the time Higgins disappeared, they were tired and maybe a little relieved that he was gone. He's got a sister and a brother, nieces and nephews. All still live in Carbondale. Mom, too. None of them made much of an effort to find him." On the verge of buttering another cracker, Jim lost his appetite and put down the knife. "I don't know what he was doing here. He doesn't seem to have any visible means of support."

"He might have been one of Dina's projects."

" 'Projects?' "

Kate nodded. "They had those cabins up the hill, empty all winter. It bothered Dina, and maybe Ruthe, too, although she used to give Dina a hard time about Dina's big idea."

"Which was?"

Kate shrugged. "Nothing major. Dina thought the cabins ought to be put to some use is all."

"So they rented them out to drifters? What the hell were two lone women, one of them getting close to feeble, doing inviting weirdos to move in up the goddamn hill from them?"

"They were careful," Kate said. "Yeah, okay, obviously not careful enough this year. But they'd been doing it for years without incident."

"They have somebody up there every winter?"

"Almost. One or two every year. They booted them out come breakup and the first paying customer."

"They stay booted?"

"Pretty much. Dina told me one time that she was giving them breathing space, a chance to find their feet. See if they liked the Park enough to stay. She said ninety percent of them didn't, and they never saw them again." She smiled.

"What?"

"They let Mac Devlin stay up there the winter his cabin burned."

"You're kidding me."

"Nope."

Jim smiled, too.

"Well, I better get back to it," Kate said.

Jim looked around. "You've done a lot. Looks almost back to normal." He noticed a little pile on the small table next to Dina's chair. "What's this?"

Kate looked. "Oh, that. I'm getting some pictures together for Dina's potlatch. They don't have much in the way of people pictures."

"When is it?"

"Saturday. At the school gym."

"Bernie'll be annoyed."

"The Roadhouse is too small. Ruthe and Dina have been here too long and have too many friends."

"I suppose." He hesitated. "Did you think about waiting?"

"For what?"

"Ruthe."

Kate paused. "Yeah," she said, "I thought about it. But . . . I don't know. Ruthe was—she is a 'fish or cut bait' kind of person. She'd say, Get it done."

"Not the sentimental type."

"No," Kate said, smiling a little. "Dina was the idealist. Ruthe is always the pragmatist. The art of the practical, that's Ruthe's specialty."

"Yeah," he said, giving the copy of *National Geographic* he held a reminiscent smile. The cover featured a story entitled "Gates of the Arctic National Park." "I remember that about her."

There was a moment of electric silence.

For no reason at all, the hair stood straight up on the

back of his neck. He looked across the table to find her eyes fixed on him, narrowed and hostile. The look pulled him to his feet, ready for fight or flight. "Kate?"

It was purely involuntary, a knee-jerk reaction. She didn't stop to think about it; she just picked up the little tin lockbox and let fly. Its arc was swift and her aim was true. The box caught him just above the left eyebrow and burst open. A paper blizzard fluttered out and down.

"Ouch!" Jim slapped a hand to his eye and rocked back a step. "That hurt! Damn it, Kate!"

"Is there a woman left in this Park you *haven't* slept with!" She grabbed a coffee mug and let fly with that, too.

The mug missed, which was a good thing, since he never saw it coming. He heard it slam into the sink and shatter, though. Warm fluid was running down the side of his face and obscuring his vision. He took a stumbling step forward, trying to preempt future missiles. He nearly fell over the coffee table, which movement, fortuitously for him, caused her to miss his head with the big red *Webster's Unabridged*. It hit his right shoulder instead.

"Shit!"

"What's with all the noise?" Dandy Mike said, peeking in the door, and ducked back just in time to avoid the poker. It missed Jim, striking the wall next to the door instead and landing at his feet with a clang. "Never mind, none of my business, just checking in. I'll be leaving now," said Dandy Mike, his voice barely audible over the sound of feet rapidly retreating down the stairs.

She'd snatched up an Aladdin lamp, the reservoir still half-filled with oil, when he tackled her and wrestled her onto the couch. The chimney fell off the lamp and miraculously did not break as it rolled beneath the table.

"Stop it, Kate," he said, breathing hard. "Damn it, I said stop it!"

This as she dropped the lamp and he got an elbow to the jaw that made his teeth snap together painfully. He caught her hands and pushed them into the small of her back. She head-butted him. "Ouch! Jesus!" The only way to immobilize her was to lie on her full length, which he did. It wasn't even funny how long he'd been waiting to get her horizontal and this was the only way he could get it done.

"Get off me!"

"What the hell is the matter with you!"

She tried to knee him in the groin. He shifted at the last possible minute. "Kate," he said. He was angry now. "Knock it off."

She heaved beneath him, trying to throw him off, and they both rolled to the floor, Kate on the bottom. She inhaled sharply. "Get off me!" He'd lost his grip on her hands in the fall, and she tried to hit him. He grabbed her hands again and held them over her head.

"Jesus!" he said. "What the *hell* is the matter with you!"

"Get off me, you son of a bitch! Get *off*!"

Their eyes met, hers narrow and furious, his widening as realization struck.

"You're jealous," he said.

She erupted in a fury of denial, kicking, butting, hitting, elbows, knees, feet, everything in action. "Let me go!"

He felt as if he were trying to hold on to an earthquake. "Christ! Stop it, Kate! Ouch!" This when she kicked him in the shin. "Kate!" She tried to head-butt him again. She was strong and agile, but he was bigger and getting angrier. After another attempt on his balls, he kneed her legs apart and pressed her down.

She froze. He froze. Sight of the edge of the cliff they were about to go over came to them both at the same moment, but then he'd been hard since they hit the floor.

"Kate," he said, her name an unrecognizable husk of sound. He bent his head.

"No!" She erupted again, fighting, clawing, even trying to bite him.

Maybe it was the click of her teeth in his ear. Maybe it

was just the result of all that friction. Whatever it was, something inside him slipped off the chain, something famished and feral and prowling, something totally out of his control. He could smell it, smell the need in her, the craving. It was as strong as his, as basic as his, and if it wasn't, he didn't care. He would take what he wanted anyway. His hand tightened around her wrists and she cried out. He used the other to yank up the hem of her shirt and tear off her bra. Her breasts were small and firm, the nipples hard and brown, and he took them into his mouth in turn, suckling as if he were starving. She cried out again and arched up, her body a tense bow. He slid his hand between her legs and rubbed the heel of his hand hard against her. She screamed then, in ecstasy or outrage, her body pressing into him, her head pressed against the floor, and he went for the snap of her jeans before she could start fighting him again.

But she wasn't fighting him now. She had one hand free and knotted in his hair, holding his head still while she kissed him, her teeth and tongue voracious, one hand clawing at his shirt, one leg hooked around his waist. The coffee table got in the way and she kicked it over. It smacked into the unsteady pile of paperwork leaning up against the wall and the classics dictionary came crashing to the floor, barely missing their heads.

Oblivious, she ran her teeth down the side of his neck and he nearly came then and there. "Wait, damn it, wait, wait," he said, tugging desperately at her jeans. Her hips gave a quick wriggle and the jeans slid, oh thank god, all the way down; he managed to pull them off one leg before she went for his belt. One second he was free and in the next he was caught again, driving into her, the one place he'd wanted to be for a year and a half, longer than that, an eternity of wanting, back where it was tight and hot and wet and Kate, Kate, Kate.

———

He was pretty sure she came again. He knew he had, hard enough to wonder why the floor hadn't splintered beneath them. Hard enough to wonder if he'd hurt her.

Jim Chopin in the sack was all about control, all about subtlety and skill and patience. He liked women, and he was self-aware enough to know that he was one up on most men in that he didn't fear them, either. He liked the getting and giving of mutual pleasure, mutually arrived at, mutually satisfying. He was proud of that, taking a certain amount of smug satisfaction in his expertise. He was not into pain, he liked to take his time, and it just wasn't any fun if his partner wasn't enjoying herself as much as he was. Life was too short to have bad sex.

But this time, this one time, he had been hasty, rough, and reckless, frantic to get at her, ridden by a red devil of lust that whipped him on and over the edge into madness. This time, he had displayed all the refinement and sophistication of a moose in rut. This time, he still had most of his clothes on.

So much for control. So much for finesse. Ah, shit.

He summoned the strength from somewhere and raised his head to look down at her. Her eyes were closed, her neat cap of hair a tangled dark halo. Her lips were swollen and parted as she gulped in air. A pulse beat frantically at the base of her throat, and he couldn't resist—he had to bend his head and settle his mouth over it, sucking at the warm, throbbing lifeblood beneath the skin. He could hear her breathing. He could feel her hands on his back, the sting of the scratches she'd left there. She radiated heat like a furnace. He could smell her, the aroma that to him was redolent of a cold draft beer after a long, hot day, a piece of Auntie Vi's fry bread, Bobby's special caribou steaks, quick-fried in hot oil and then baked in a wine and cream sauce, a shot of Ruthe's framboise—every good thing to eat and drink he'd ever had in his life, that's what Kate Shugak smelled like to Jim Chopin. Her pulse beat against his tongue and he wanted to eat her alive. For the first time, he understood the eroticism underlying the story of Dracula, and the unexpected thought made him laugh low in his throat.

He felt her lashes flutter, and he looked up, to see her eyes open.

"Hey," he said, gentling his voice.

She didn't say anything, and that scared him.

"I'm sorry I was so rough." He traced a finger down her cheek. There was blood. It was his, from his temple, where she'd connected with the box. It didn't seem to matter much now. "Did I hurt you?"

"No," she said, her voice a thread of sound.

"Good." He lowered his head and kissed her slowly, deeply, thoroughly, feeling himself begin to harden inside her again. Jesus, he thought, not again, no way, not this quick. Not since I was fifteen anyway. He was more than willing to go with it, though, until he felt her hand against his chest, pushing, and raised his head again. "What?"

"No," she said again, and pushed him off her to wriggle free. She caught him unawares and he rolled into the coffee table, catching the back of his head on a corner.

"Ouch! Damn it!" He grabbed the back of his head. "Didn't we do this already?"

She didn't apologize, just reached for her clothes and skinnied into them as fast as she could.

"Kate." She didn't answer. "Kate," he said, rising to his feet. He'd lost his tie, one shoulder seam of his shirt was ripped, and he had to grab at his pants before they fell down. "What's wrong?"

She gave him a hunted look. "Nothing's wrong. I have to go is all. Where's my other shoe?"

"Kate." He reached for her and she stepped quickly out of range. "Wait."

"No. This can't happen."

"Why not?" he said, starting to get angry again and trying

to tamp it down. He'd just had the most exciting sexual experience of his life and now the cause of it was about to walk out the door. He didn't like it. He didn't like it one little bit. "And I'm pretty sure it already did."

"It was a mistake." She swallowed and shoved the hair out of her face. "I shouldn't have thrown the box at you. I—I shouldn't have done a lot of things. I—I'm sorry, I have to go."

"Like hell!" He reached for her again and would have caught her if he hadn't stumbled over her other shoe.

"Oh, good," she said, and scooped it up. Gal hissed from the loft, to which she had retreated when the shooting war began. Kate retrieved her and tucked her inside her parka.

"Kate, don't go!"

The slam of the door was her reply. The cabin shook beneath the weight of her hasty steps on the stairs. Her snow machine roared into life a moment later, followed by a surprised yip, probably from Mutt.

"Shit!" Jim said. His left eye had crusted over so that he could barely see out of it. "Shit," he repeated. "Shit, shit, shit."

He cleaned himself up as best he could, checking his reflection in the little mirror on the kitchen wall. Yeah, he was going to have a shiner. His shoulder was sore, too. He thought at first it was from where she had hit him with the dictionary, until he investigated and saw the teeth marks. He didn't even remember her biting him.

Well, his uniform was going to require some serious rehab. "Not to mention my life," he said out loud. He sighed heavily and began to clean up, stacking the papers back beneath the dictionary, righting the table, picking up the papers that had scattered from the tin lockbox.

One caught his attention, a thick piece of parchment beginning to turn yellow with age. He read it twice, disbelieving his eyes, and a third time, just to be sure.

"Jesus Christ," he said blankly. He stared around the

room as if he'd never seen it before. He read the piece of paper again. Was this a joke? This had to be a joke. "Jesus H. Roosevelt Christ."

The door opened. Dandy Mike peeped in. "Is it safe to come in now? It's freezing out here."

"What?" Jim remembered Dandy poking his head in the door in the middle of his very own personal firestorm. "Oh. Yeah. Sure. Hey."

"Hey yourself." Dandy sidled inside and cast a wary look around. He seemed surprised at the relative order that reigned inside the little cabin. "I saw Kate leaving, so I figured it was safe to come up."

Oh no. "Were you outside all this time?"

Dandy's eyes slid away. "No. Well, kinda. Well, okay, yeah, I was. What was she so mad about anyway?"

Dandy Mike was, Jim's own activities in that field notwithstanding, the biggest rounder in the Park. He knew women. There was nothing wrong with his hearing, either. Jim repressed a sigh. It'd be all over the Park before sunset, which on this day was less than an hour away. One more thing for Kate to be pissed about.

Although, now that he thought about it . . . Jim felt a smile spread slowly across his face. If word got at least as far as Ethan Int-Hout, that would be okay with him.

"Jim?" Dandy said.

"What are you doing here anyway, Dandy?"

"Who, me? Oh, I don't know, I heard you were in town, and I figured you'd be up here, and, you know, I was first on the scene, so I . . ." His voice trailed off when he noticed Jim's stare. "Well, I wondered if you could use some help is all. I can see you had help, so I'll go."

"Dandy."

Dandy stopped, his hand on the door.

"What's up?"

Dandy turned, pulling off his knit cap and examining the

brim as if his soul depended on an even rib stitch. "I hear you're moving your post to the Park."

Oh, hell. Billy Mike hadn't waited to spread the word, and who would he tell but his own son? His own chronically out-of-work son. "News travels fast."

"Yeah. So I was wondering . . ."

"Wondering what?"

Dandy shifted his weight. "Well, if maybe you'd be hiring. Like, I don't know, an assistant."

Jim was momentarily dumbfounded. "You want a job?" he said, heavily stressing the first and last words.

Dandy flushed. "Well, I might. Maybe. I guess. Yes." He shifted his feet. "I'm thinking about getting married, and—"

Jim stared at him. "I beg your pardon?" Dandy started to speak, but Jim waved him to silence. There was nothing wrong with Jim's hearing, either. "Never mind, I don't think I'll still be standing if I hear it twice."

He took a long look at the floor, vaguely surprised that there wasn't a charred outline of his and Kate's bodies marking the spot. He still wasn't sure he hadn't died and gone to heaven right there.

"I've got some calls to make. Let's head back into town."

7

Kate had given a potlatch for her grandmother. This would be her second, and she felt relatively experienced. The place—the gym—was set and the principal was declining rent. "Even if their, er, lifestyle wasn't one that we would want to set up as an example for the children," she told Kate, and since the woman hadn't been in the Park even a year and was totally clueless, Kate forbore to snarl.

There had to be a lot of food, but everyone would bring a dish, so all Kate had to do was make sure there was pop and that it was cold. George had promised to fill up a plane and would only charge for freight. She had coerced the senior class into filling half a dozen coolers with snow.

There ought to be gifts to give away, things that would remind the guests of Dina. That was more difficult, especially since Ruthe was still hanging on to life by a thread in the Chief William Memorial Hospital in Ahtna, and Kate did not know which of Dina's possessions Ruthe would want to keep.

Kate had flown to Ahtna two days before, to sit vigil next

to Ruthe, a figure swathed in bandages, hooked up to enough machines to launch a space shuttle. One was breathing for her. The doctor, who was personally acquainted with Kate Shugak's built-in bullshit detector, was very frank. "We've done all we can. It's up to her now."

So Kate settled into an uncomfortable armchair and read out loud for two hours, parts of *Travels with Charley, The Monkey Wrench Gang,* and even a few entries out of *Alaska's Wilderness Medicines.* She thought Ruthe had given a tiny smile when she read the entry on devil's club, but it could have been her imagination.

Her shift ended and Chick's began. He had a nice mellow baritone and sang a pretty good folk song. Kate listened at the door to a few lines of "The Unfortunate Miss Bailey" before Mandy materialized in front of her with cups of coffee. They sat together in the lounge. "You headed back home?" Mandy said. She was a rangy woman with short, prematurely graying hair and skin weathered by long days in the Arctic sun.

Kate nodded. "I've got the potlatch to get ready for."

"Yeah. We'll be back for that."

Kate looked at Ruthe lying in the bed, unmoving. "Is the whole Park coming to Ahtna in shifts?"

"Kind of looks like it. Auntie Joy was with her when we got here, but then, she lives right down the road." In Alaskan terms, "right down the road" meaning within seventy miles. "I think people are just showing up. Dan O'Brian said he'd bring a copy of d-2 and read it to her."

"That'll bring her back," Kate said, and both women smiled.

"What's this I hear about Dan being forced to retire?"

Kate shook her head. "Not going to happen. I sicked Auntie Vi on it."

"Well, if anyone can get the job done."

"Yeah. Did I hear correctly—that he was standing over the bodies when Dandy walked in?" Mandy continued.

"Yeah. He'd stopped by to ask them for help with his job."

"Wow." Mandy expelled a breath. "He must have almost walked in on whoever did it."

"I wish he had." Mandy was avoiding Kate's eyes. Now Kate remembered how Dandy Mike had stared at her, open-mouthed, as she had rushed by on her way to her snow machine. "What?"

Mandy shrugged uncomfortably. "Dandy's been saying some stuff."

Kate's shoulders tensed. "About me and Jim Chopin?" she said, keeping her voice even.

"Yeah. At Dina and Ruthe's cabin. He said you were fighting."

Kate stared. "What?"

"He said you were fighting. Well, he said you were using Jim for target practice. And I saw Jim at the post office in Niniltna yesterday; he's got a shiner. A beauty."

"He does?"

Mandy smiled. "Yes. He does."

Kate felt herself relaxing. "Oh. Ah. Well."

"Why'd you hit him?"

"Because he deserved it," Kate said swiftly, if inaccurately.

"What, did he try to make a move?"

Kate didn't know what to say without giving herself away. Mandy had been too close a friend for too long. Fortunately for Kate, Mandy decided to answer herself. "Like he never did that before."

"Right," Kate said. "Did you mush into Ahtna?"

Mandy shook her head. "No." She was still curious. She'd never heard of Jim Chopin pressing unwanted advances on anyone. He'd never had to—most women crumbled at the first long look, the first smile that said, I know you. Let me show you how well. And Mandy did know Kate Shugak better than most. Enough to know when the NO TRESPASSING sign was out. "No place to kennel the dogs."

"Who's taking care of them while you're gone?"

"Didn't he tell you?"

"No," Kate said, "no, he didn't tell me anything." She caught Mandy's look and said, "I'm sorry. "Who?"

"Johnny. Johnny's stopping by on his way to and from school to take care of the dogs."

"No kidding. He know what he's doing?"

Mandy reflected. "More or less."

"You paying him?"

"More or less. He wants to learn to mush."

"He wants to learn everything," Kate said.

They smiled at each other. The little lost boy, did he but know it, was lost no more.

On Saturday, before the potlatch, Kate went back up to the Step. Dan was sitting behind his desk. "Hey, Kate."

She surveyed him critically as she took a seat. "You don't look as peaked as you did the last time I saw you. The bruise is fading."

"Yeah." He rubbed his head. "That Dandy throws a mean door."

Kate laughed and tossed him a bag. "Here, couple pieces of Auntie Vi's fry bread. They're cold, but you can nuke 'em."

"Marry me," Dan said, and took her advice and popped them in the microwave. "Almost as good as right out of the pan," he managed to say around a mouthful. "If you won't marry me, I'm trying for Auntie Vi."

"Have you heard anything?"

"About the job? I'm still suspended."

"I notice you're also still here."

"Yeah," he said, and grinned. It did her heart good to see it. "I got a couple of calls—none from my boss—saying I should stick it out and make 'em fire me. The thing is, Kate . . ."

"What?"

He brushed crumbs from his shirt. "The Park Service subsists on a budget set every two years by Congress, just like every other government bureaucracy. The funds within that bureaucracy are allocated, allegedly, on a case-per-case basis, according to greatest need. Unless there are specific congressional requirements that set aside particular funding for any given project, the money goes into a general operating budget. And that budget is overseen by the secretary of the interior, who handpicks his or her staff members, one of whom is my boss. The secretary, you will note, is a political appointee, who serves at the whim of the president, a president who can fire his or her ass."

"I got it, Dan. I think I had it before I sat down."

"Yeah, well, I just don't want the Park to suffer because the secretary or one of her minions doesn't happen to like the chief ranger. And hell, it's not like I wouldn't want my own people in charge if I were taking over." He brooded. "Ah hell. I figure whatever happens, I'll deal with it."

"Good attitude. In the meantime, what's going on?"

"What's going on is that all the bears are asleep, the moose are bedded down by the rivers, conserving energy, and the Kanuyaq caribou will start getting thinned down"—he looked at the calendar—"in four days, which will considerably relieve my mind. Other than that, there isn't much going on. Have to start going through applications for summer hires. Shovel some snow off the roof."

"You lonely up here all by yourself?"

He shrugged. "No." His grin was sly this time. "Course, I'm not up here all by myself all the time."

Kate rolled her eyes. "Right. What was I thinking. How's Christie?"

"Perfect." But he didn't look as smug as he ought to have when he said it.

"Trouble in paradise?" she said lightly.

He crumpled the paper bag and tossed it in the trash.

Then the in box needed straightening. "No," he said. "No trouble."

Okay. "See you at the potluck?"

His brow lightened. "I'll be down."

"Good. Because you know the fry bread was just an appetizer."

It got a smile out of him, but Kate worried about him all the way down from the Step.

It beat worrying about herself.

She opened the doors to the gymnasium at precisely 12:00 P.M., and people began to stream inside. Dandy Mike had come early and helped her set up the long tables that lined the front of the cafeteria window. Fortunately, he also knew the secret to making the bleachers come out of the wall, because Kate certainly didn't. The coolers were beneath the tables, loaded with six different kinds of pop. The tabletops were soon obscured beneath a layer of meat loaf, macaroni and cheese, blood stew, cinnamon rolls, seventeen different kinds of fruit bread as well as innumerable loaves of homemade white bread, caribou ribs, moose roast, and the last silver of someone's fishing season, rescued from the cache and roasted whole. There were enormous bowls of mashed potatoes and boiled carrots, along with bean salad, macaroni salad, fruit salad, carrot salad, and five different kinds of coleslaw. There were sheet cakes and layer cakes, pumpkin, apple, and cherry pies, brownies, angel bars, and homemade butterscotch candy. They'd done Dina proud.

Kate kept up with the napkins and the plastic flatware while exchanging greetings with the people filling their plates on the other side of the table. Knots of people gathered on the bleachers, and more people streamed in, then more, and the hum of conversation became first a din and then a roar. It wasn't long before the little kids found the basketball closet and began practicing free throws at the opposite end of the court.

At 1:30, the drummers assembled onstage and the room quieted momentarily. "Hey, everybody," Wilson Mike said, raising drum and stick, and "Hey, Wilson," everybody said back.

"We're singing for Dina today," Wilson said, "and you're dancing," and before he struck the second note and the singers got started on their first song, people were out in the middle of the gym floor, shoes off, feet moving and finger fans counting the beat. Everybody had on winter clothes, so it wasn't long before they started sweating, too. It was noisy, and for the most part not very graceful, and filled with joy. It lifted Kate's heart to see it.

She was behind a table, dispensing gifts. Well, one gift, the same gift over and over, a reprint of the group photo taken at the Kanuyaq Mine those many years ago. She'd gotten the owner of the Ahtna Photo Shop out of bed on her trip in to see Ruthe and had him make up a negative and run two hundred prints, then bullied him further into doing a rush order from Anchorage on some wooden frames. They weren't all the same frame, but the picture was going over very well. "Ayapu," Auntie Vi said. "That the time that man Smith, he flying tourists to the mine from Cordova." She was silent, looking at the photograph. The frame she had picked was dark blue wood, and it set off the black-and-white photograph very well. "Ekaterina, she look so young. Dina, and Ruthe, too. And Ray Chevak, hmm, yes." She cast Kate a sideways glance. "You know Ray Chevak?"

Kate, unruffled, said, "I met him in Bering this summer."

Auntie Vi nodded. "I go dance now."

"Knock 'em dead, Auntie," Kate said, and shooed her off. Billy Mike met Auntie Vi halfway and matched her steps into the circle.

One thing you could say for Park rats, they sure did love to dance. All ages, all sexes, all sizes, they were, to a man and a woman, dancing fools. There was no such thing as a wallflower in Niniltna, of either sex. It helped that most of the time the dancing was Native, en masse and the more the merrier. You could dance with one partner or twenty, but the one thing you never had to do was dance alone.

She turned, bumping into Pete Heiman as she did. "Well, hey, Pete, just the guy I wanted to see. I hoped you'd be here this afternoon."

He laughed. "I'm afraid, very afraid."

"Step into my office," Kate said, and led the way through a side door.

Outside, the snow was falling in small soft flakes. Kate heard a plane take off but couldn't see it. There were some men clustered together at the end of the building, sharing a bottle. Kate repressed the urge to glare at them and looked back at Pete.

Pete lit a cigarette. "What's up, Kate?" Through the smoke, his eyes were watchful.

His eyes were always watchful. Pete Heiman was the duly elected senator for District 41, which included the Park, and, as such, every Park rat's Juneau mouthpiece. He was also an old drinking buddy of Abel's, and Kate had known him all her life. She liked him, but she didn't trust him. Still, he was her mouthpiece, too. "Dan O'Brian's been suspended as chief ranger for the Park. They're trying to pressure him into early retirement."

"Dan the ranger." Pete drew on his cigarette. "Well, well. I hadn't heard."

"You're a little slower than usual on the uptake, then, it's all over the Park. No one wants him to go, Pete. Can you call someone?"

Pete had run for reelection that fall, and Kate had worked for his opponent, who had almost beaten him and would have if a couple of nasty little murders hadn't gotten in the way, so technically he was under no obligation to grant Kate a favor. On the other hand, this was Kate Shugak asking him a favor. Kate could all but hear the gears ticking over between Pete's ears.

"Whom would you suggest I call?"

He was stalling, and they both knew it. Pete Heiman had been a card-carrying Republican from his cradle; his father and his grandfather had seen to that. If he didn't know whom to call, nobody did. "I've got people working the phones here, too," Kate said.

"Which people?"

"Just people," Kate said. "Come on, Pete. You know you have to. If you don't, you'll be the only one who doesn't, and where does that put you? Better it sounds like it's your idea."

"Are you under the impression that I owe you anything?"

"No. No, I'm not."

"So then you'd owe me."

"Careful," Kate said, opening the door. "The last person who said that to me is dead."

Inside, he caught her arm. "Who's that blonde?" He nodded at Christie Turner, who was dancing next to Dandy Mike in the circle.

"Bernie's new barmaid."

The song was thundering to a finish. "Introduce us."

"Bernie will kill me," Kate muttered. "Not to mention Dan." But she did as she was told, a down payment on the payback.

Christie accepted an invitation to dance, and since the drummers were taking a break, Pete guided her to a chair instead and brought her a plateful of choice morsels. Kate, watching from behind the gift table, saw the infamous Heiman charm begin to have its inevitable effect. Pete had a weakness for blondes, having married three of them. She hoped Christie had the backbone to resist, because Pete's ego was already big enough. Plus, he had to be at least thirty

years her senior, not to mention her prior relationship with
Dan. Where was Dan? She looked around but didn't see
him.

"Kate."

She stiffened. "Jim."

"Thought I'd drop by to pay my respects." It was politic
for the resident trooper to put in an appearance at big cer-
emonial events, something in the way of a diplomatic mis-
sion. And he'd known and liked Dina. And he'd known
Kate would be there.

He looked at the picture in its many frames. "Nice idea."
He picked a dark blue one and slipped it into an inside
pocket. "I wondered how you'd get around the gift thing."

She took a careful breath. "People seem to like them.
And I didn't want to give any of Dina's stuff away. Have
you talked to the hospital today?"

He nodded. "The same."

When he looked at her, she saw a fading corner-shaped
bruise on his left temple. She hugged her elbows, caught in
a sudden draft. Or so she told herself. "How long can she
stay like that?"

"She's not in pain."

"How do we know that?"

"We don't."

"Then don't say it."

"Sorry."

There was a pause, broken by her stomach growling.

"Are you hungry?" he said.

"No." Her stomach growled again.

"I'll get us plates." He walked away.

I'll get us plates. I'll get *us* plates. Whichever way you
looked at it, the phrase made her nervous.

As if she had conjured him up, Ethan materialized in
front of her, Johnny in tow. "Hey." He leaned over to kiss
her just as Jim came back. Kate turned so that she caught
the kiss on her cheek. Ethan's eyes narrowed. Jim handed
one plate to Kate, and smiled at Ethan. Ethan didn't smile

back. "Kate," Ethan said, "I've got to talk to you."

"I'm kind of busy, Ethan." Just then, the drummers started up again and circles formed on the floor. Johnny said hopefully, "Um, will you teach me to dance?"

"Sure!" Kate said, and followed him to the floor, trying not to run.

Jim sat down and put the second plate to one side. "I'll just keep this for Kate," he said to Ethan, and began to eat under Ethan's baleful glare. "You should eat, Ethan. There's some great stuff on the table."

"Stay away from her," Ethan said.

Well now, Jim thought. It seemed that Ethan didn't know that Jim had recently been where no Ethan had gone before. He wondered why Dandy Mike was holding his fire. Probably hoping that it would get him a job. "That's her choice," he said.

"Stay away from her, goddamn it."

Jim smiled at him again, and it was about as friendly an expression as it had been before. "You're still married, aren't you, Ethan?" He watched with interest as Ethan's fair skin flushed right up to the roots of his hair. "You thinking you can have your cake and eat it, too? If so, you don't know your women." He took a ruminative bite of macaroni and cheese casserole, then added in a voice as patronizing and as patriarchal as he could make it, "But then, I never thought you did."

For a moment, he hoped he might have gone too far, but no. Ethan regrouped and gave him a contemptuous look. "Big talk from the man with the badge."

Oh. Right. He was in uniform. "Happy to take it off for the duration, Ethan," he said softly. "Just for you."

"Fuck you," Ethan said after a simmering moment, and stalked away.

"He doesn't appear to like you," said Pete Heiman, who was sitting next to Jim with Bernie's new barmaid, whose big blue eyes were even bigger and bluer than usual.

"He sure doesn't," she said. Her voice was light and breathy, perhaps consciously so, and her gaze was languishing. Jim looked at her and, as an experiment, tried to exercise the inner muscle that always used to come into play when he was faced with a pretty woman. Nothing. He was appreciative but not covetous. Interesting. But not as alarming as it had been.

He returned to his plate, his appetite good.

Meanwhile, out on the dance floor, Bobby Clark had joined Kate and Johnny. As his wheelchair rolled back and forth to the beat, Dinah danced around all three of them with Katya, who was in a backpack, waving a rattle. Mandy and Chick were down the circle a bit, Mac Devlin was doing his usual lumbering grizzly bear impression, and Bernie and Edith were jitterbugging, which was an interesting, though obviously not impossible, exercise to the beat of Native drums.

The drums beat once, twice, three times, each time harder and louder than the time before, and a cheer went up from the gymnasium floor when the last one struck. Kate handed Johnny over to Auntie Vi, from whom he would learn the smoothest moves, and went to the microphone set up at one side of the stage. "Hello the Park," she said.

"Hello!" the crowd shouted back.

"We're here today to honor the memory of one of our own. You know who I mean."

"Dina!" they answered with one voice.

"That's right, Dina Willner. She died a week ago yesterday, and we'll miss her. But we'll never forget her. And this is why."

Kate primed the pump by telling the story of Dina teaching her to rappel. She told it well, keeping it light and at her own expense, and everyone laughed.

She was followed to the microphone by Mac Devlin, who glowered out at the crowd from beneath wiry red brows and growled, "God knows, Dina and me hardly ever agreed on nothing. She was a greenie from the word go, and I think the best thing you can do with a tree is cut it down and make something out of it somebody can eat off of or sit down on. But"—he fixed the crowd with a gimlet eye— "she weren't no stealth greenie. What she was and what she believed was right out front for everybody to see, and she fought clean. I won't go so far as to say I'll miss her, but I respected her." He added gruffly, "And she was a good friend to everyone in the Park, whether you agreed with her or not. My house burned down and she was first to step forward and offer me a place to stay until I got rebuilt. She was a good friend to the Park," he repeated. "Nobody can say better than that."

Kate eased from the stage as Auntie Vi followed Mac. "Alaka, that Dina," Auntie Vi said, and everyone laughed just from the expression on her animated face. "I remember that time of ANCSA and we all go to Washington, D.C., when Dina gets into a fight with the secretary of the interior. Ayapu, she thinks she's Muhammad Ali, that girl—"

Kate moved over to lean against the wall. "Here," Jim said, handing her a plate. "Eat."

Kate's stomach was still growling and the plate was heaped with all manner of good things, so she took it, but she managed to get her mouth so full that her "Thanks" was barely audible.

"You know that lockbox you beaned me with?" He watched her as he said the words. One of the minor annoyances with being hung up on someone with brown skin was she might be blushing and you'd never know it. "It had some interesting paperwork in it."

"Oh?" Kate said, her voice uncompromising in the extreme.

"Private paperwork."

"What kind?"

He looked down at her, mostly because he was almost two feet taller than she was. "Did you know Dina had been married?"

Kate choked on a mouthful of macaroni and cheese. She coughed, then coughed again. She was making so much noise, she was interfering with the current speaker, Bernie, who was telling the tale of Dina teaching him how to make a bean drink. "Dina insisted on celery salt," he was saying, "and you had to pour a little of the water from the jar of pickled beans into the glass, too. The only trouble was that she was usually half in the bag by the time she developed an ambition to come around to my side of the bar, and she used about a half a fifth of Absolut while she was at it, which meant there wasn't a whole hell of a lot of room left for the bean juice. So she'd drink off the vodka. And then, of course, she'd have to top off the drink." He paused, then added, "She was without a doubt the worst bartender I've ever not employed."

Kate took the same side door she'd led Pete through. Once outside, she coughed some more and then sneezed violently twice in succession. Her eyes were tearing when finally, wheezing, she said, "What?"

"I guess you didn't," Jim said, handing her a napkin. She mopped her tears and blew her nose. "I found a marriage certificate. You'll never guess who to."

She looked at him.

"John Letourneau."

She gaped at him.

He nodded. "Yeah."

"But I thought—Ruthe and Dina—"

"Yeah," he repeated. "So thought we all."

She remembered, and her eyes narrowed in a way that was reminiscent enough to put him on alert. "But you—"

"Yeah." He refused to apologize. He and Ruthe had been consenting adults. Further, he refused to kiss and tell. "I was new to the Park. I didn't hear they were a couple until after. She never said. There's something else."

Kate couldn't begin to imagine what else. "What, Dina owned stock in Exxon?" It was about as believable. She remembered the two beds in Ruthe and Dina's loft. But they were in their seventies. A lot of older couples chose to sleep alone, sometimes even in separate bedrooms.

He laughed. "No, nothing that bad." He sobered. "Kate, I'm wondering about Higgins."

"The guy you caught with the murder weapon in his hand?"

"I know," he said, "I know. I've got him locked up in Tok. Would you fly up with me and talk to him, tell me what you think?"

Kate was taken aback. "You're asking me for a consultation on a closed case?"

"Maybe it isn't closed."

"Oh, let me guess. He says he didn't do it."

"He says he doesn't know, but, since I caught him with the knife, he figures he probably did."

"How original."

"The Carbondale chief sent me his sheet. There's no history of violence, none, not ever."

"What about his war record? His time in Vietnam?"

He shook his head. "None that they caught him at." "Just talk to him," Jim said. "I'd like to have your opinion." He paused. "Please."

The "Please" unnerved her, knocked her off balance. She opened the door and peered inside.

Pete was at the mike, talking about the time Dina lobbied the Juneau legislature to pass the permanent-fund dividend. "The woman never bought a drink," he was saying; "she thought that's what legislators were for."

But the potlatch was winding down. Christie was sitting on the edge of the stage, holding court. Kate didn't see Dan. A line had already formed in the cafeteria kitchen to wash the dishes, people were shrugging into coats, stamping into boots, and rounding up children, and the drummers had packed up. She could make sure Johnny didn't go home without escort, ask Auntie Vi to oversee the cleanup. Avoid Ethan.

"I'll get my coat," she said.

It was snowing still, but visibility was good and the flight was quick. That was fine with Kate. It wasn't that she was nervous at rubbing elbows with him for a hundred miles, she assured herself, it was the close quarters with a man who, when you came right down to it, she barely knew. Whom she barely knew enough to bean with a lockbox. Whom she didn't know anywhere well enough to sleep with.

I am losing my mind, she thought.

Halfway to Tok, he broke the increasingly heavy silence. "I don't suppose this could qualify as our first date?"

Kate didn't reply, and she was out of the Cessna the moment it rolled to a halt on the Tok airstrip. She helped him push it into its parking space, keeping on the opposite side of the fuselage he was on. The journey to the post was accomplished in silence.

Higgins was curled up on the bed of the cell. He looked cleaner and certainly smelled better than he had the last time Jim had seen him. It was always amazing, the difference a shower and a couple of meals made in a suspect. Jim remembered a conversation he'd had with a woman he had dated a while back who had taught remedial English to guests of the state going for their GEDs. "I read about the horrible things they do in the papers, and then I meet them and they seem so nice, so polite," she'd told him. "They don't seem like monsters. Why are they so different once they're in prison?"

"For one thing, they're sober," he'd told her.

But Higgins hadn't been drunk, or high, the day he'd killed Dina, the day he'd put Ruthe in the hospital. His tox screen had come back clean as a whistle.

Higgins rolled over to look at them when Jim called his name, then rolled right back again. "Come on, Riley," Jim said. "Sit up, would you? I've got someone here I'd like you to meet."

"Does he have an attorney?" Kate said in a low voice.

"Hasn't asked for one."

She raised an eyebrow. They both knew from bitter experience that a perp without an attorney was a confession just waiting to be kicked. Defense attorneys were as much witness to due process as they were advocate for the accused.

"I know," Jim said, "but I can't force one on him." He raised his voice. "Riley?"

Kate silenced him with an upraised hand. She pointed to the door. Jim frowned and shook his head. She kept pointing. He sighed, handed her the key, and stepped into the hall. He left Mutt behind, though.

"Mr. Higgins." Kate kept her voice low and calm. "May I please come in?"

The novelty of being asked permission to enter his jail cell did not fail to have an effect. Higgins rolled to a sitting position and looked at her with anxious eyes. "Do I know you?"

"No, sir, we haven't met. My name is Kate Shugak." She let her hand rest on Mutt's head. "This is Mutt."

He met Mutt's yellow stare and smiled. "What a beautiful dog." He reached a hand through the bars. Kate tensed and almost warned him, and then his hand was scratching Mutt between the ears and the big gray half wolf was leaning into it.

There was a dead silence. Kate pulled herself together enough to say, "May I come in, Mr. Higgins?"

"The door's locked," he said apologetically, as if she wouldn't know that, and as if he were committing some dreadful social solecism by confessing to it.

"I have a key. May I?"

"Oh. Certainly." He rose to his feet as she entered, Mutt padding at her side. There was a chair opposite the bunk, next to the sink. The jail kept its cells clean, but there were some smells you can never scrub away, and human vomit, urine, and excrement were three of the most pervasive. Kate sat down in the chair. Higgins waited until she was seated before sitting on the bunk. He had awfully good manners for a murderer.

His dark hair was thinning and cut to above his ears, his face gaunt, lined, and freshly shaven. His hands, clasped in front of him, were large-knuckled and scarred. He was so thin, his body was little more than a layer of skin over bone. He was probably fifty, fifty-five. He looked a hundred.

"You're from Illinois, I understand, Mr. Higgins."

He looked startled. "Yes, I am. Carbondale."

"All your life?"

"Yes. Well, except for when I was in the army." He ducked his head. "You know what the worst thing about jail is?"

"What?"

"No windows. In the movies, there are always windows, with bars on, that you can see out of."

"With John Wayne on the other side."

He smiled, delighted that she would play. "Right."

"That was always in Texas. Be cold here."

He frowned. "Oh, I guess. I hadn't thought about it."

"It's a long way from Illinois to Alaska."

"Yes. I mean, I guess so."

"A long drive for someone traveling alone."

He looked away. "I walked."

The AlCan was fifteen hundred miles long, plus however many miles it was from Milepost Zero to Carbondale, Illinois. "Hitchhiked, do you mean?"

"Yeah, that's what I mean," he said too quickly.

She nodded. By now, it would be next to impossible to find anyone who had given him a ride, even if his story were true, which it wasn't. "That's quite a trip. You must have seen some country."

"Oh, yeah," he said, his face lighting. "Beautiful. Like nothing I've ever seen. I've never been anywhere before, just home, and—well, just home, really. This was like—this was—" He shrugged and spread his hands. "Amazing."

"Yeah," she said, "I've heard."

"You've never driven it yourself?"

She shook her head. "The two times I've been Outside, I flew."

"You ought to drive it," he said earnestly. "At least once."

"I've been told that," she said, nodding. She let the amiable silence lie between them for a moment or two. "So the Park was the first left turn after you crossed the border," she said, smiling at him. Kate's smile, while not as lethal as Jim Chopin's, seldom failed to have an effect, either.

He smiled back. "Well, maybe not the first turn. But one of them."

"It's a hard place to pass up. I know. I've lived here most of my life."

"I wondered." He gave her a curious look. "If you don't mind my asking, are you an Indian?"

"I don't mind," Kate said, "and no, I'm an Alaska Native. Aleut, mostly, but if you go back a generation or two, it's quite a mix. Pretty much everyone who dropped by Alaska dipped their pen in my ancestors' inkwell, from the Russians on down. Heinz fifty-seven American."

Mutt lay down, and again Higgins scratched her head and retained his hand, and again Mutt leaned into it, as opposed to moving out of the way or even just tolerating it.

"Just about the most beautiful dog I've ever seen," Higgins said quietly.

"She's half wolf," Kate said.

His eyes widened. "Really?" He looked back at Mutt. "Wow. She seems pretty civilized. I always thought wolf hybrids were dangerous around people."

"Mutt's the exception. And she's got a pretty big backyard to run off any aggression she might be feeling." Although the aggression was always there, and on tap when it was needed.

"Where did you get her?"

"She was a gift." Kate nudged the conversation back on track. "Must have been tough, your first winter in the Park."

"It wasn't that bad," he said. "I met Dina and Ruthe at the Roadhouse, and they were looking for someone to do odd jobs around their place for the winter. Cut wood, like that."

Kate nodded. "Yeah, they're always looking for someone. Not many can stick out an Interior winter, when they've just gotten here."

"Yeah, your fall doesn't last long," he said, nodding. "I got here and, *bam!* it snowed. It was early compared to home. I was surprised."

The first snowfall had been on October 17. "And then it kept snowing."

"For six days," he said ruefully, "and Dina and Ruthe had a heck of a lot of path to shovel."

"Nice little cabins, up the hill."

"Yeah," he said nostalgically. "And an incredible view. Dina said that on a clear day you can see all the way to Prince William Sound. But I think she was fooling me."

"That why you killed her?" Kate said, asking her first question of the interview.

His head snapped up and he stared at her out of wounded eyes. "I don't know," he said, his voice strained.

"You mean you didn't kill her? You didn't try to kill Ruthe?"

"I don't know. The way he found me, I must have—" He closed his eyes and what little flesh was left seemed to melt away from his face. "I don't remember doing it, but I must have," he whispered.

"Ever do anything like this before?"

"I don't know. Sometimes—"

"Sometimes what?"

"Sometimes I lose time."

"You lose time?"

"I just blank out. One minute I'm walking down the street, and the sun's out, and the kids are playing in the school yard, and the next minute I'm in the shelter, lying on a bed, wrapped up in a blanket."

"You had the knife in your hand when you were found. Did you blank that out, too?"

"I don't remember any knife," he said helplessly. "I don't remember anything after—" He stopped.

"After what?"

He didn't answer.

"If you didn't kill Dina, who did?"

"I don't know!"

"Pretty convenient, your not knowing."

"*I don't know!* Oh god! Oh god!" He moaned and put his hands over his ears. "Can you hear it? Can you hear it?"

"Hear what?"

"They're coming!"

"Who's coming?"

"Incoming!" he screamed, and took her down in a diving tackle. Mutt was on her feet in an instant, barking wildly.

Jim was through the door a heartbeat later, to find Higgins trying to drag Kate beneath his bunk, screaming *"Incoming! Incoming!"* at the top of his voice. Kate was trying to fight him off, and Mutt had her teeth fastened on the back of Kate's sweatshirt and was pulling with her legs braced, growling all the time.

She let go as soon as she saw Jim and started barking. The cement walls of the cells rang like a tocsin. Jim got one arm around Kate's waist and hauled her up. For a moment, Higgins wouldn't let go, and then he did and scuttled beneath his bunk. Jim deposited Kate unceremoniously in the hallway, said, "Out!" to Mutt, and went back into the cell. Higgins was curled into a ball, his knees to his chest and his arms over his head, moaning and crying and sobbing. "Oh God, I'm so scared, I'm so scared. Make it stop. Make it stop. Make it *stop!*"

"Riley," Jim said. Higgins kept rocking and moaning. "Riley. Riley! It's all over. The attack's over, Riley. It's safe to come out now."

Higgins's sobbing slowly ceased.

"Come on, Riley." Jim held out a hand. He could hear Higgins snorting back mucus.

"I'm going to stay here for a while. If that's okay?"

"Sure," Jim said. "Sure it is." He pulled the blanket and the pillow off the bunk and gave them to Riley, who thanked him and proceeded to blow his nose on the blanket.

Jim stood up and left the cell, locking it behind him. He motioned to Kate, and the three of them padded silently down the hall, leaving the man beneath the bunk to crouch, shivering and terrified, waiting for the next attack.

"Poor bastard," Kate said.

"Yeah," Jim said. "But did he do it?"

———

"Poor fucker," Bobby said.

He was sitting in front of the computer, one of the many electronic components of the console that occupied the center of the A-frame. He had a satellite uplink now and was the only person in the Park, apart from Dan and the school, to have instant Internet access. He tapped some keys and a different site popped up—one with a Department of Defense logo—one Jim was not entirely certain Bobby should have been able to get on, but he held his peace.

"He was at Hue. Private Riley Higgins, Seventh Cav." He shook his head, exited, and sat back. "No wonder the poor fucker's crazy."

"I would remind you that this particular poor fucker killed Dina Willner, and may have killed Ruthe Bauman while he was at it," Kate said tartly.

"Poor pucker," Katya said sadly, trying to twist a Rubik's Cube on the floor at Bobby's feet.

"Listen to the girl, wouldja, she's talking good as her daddy!" Bobby roared, snatching up his daughter and cradling her in his arms. Katya blinked up at him, surprised, and then gave him a blinding smile and a smacking kiss.

Dinah sighed and looked at Jim and Kate. "Soup's on."

It wasn't soup; it was a big moose roast with the bone in, served with potatoes and carrots in a thick brown garlicky gravy and big hunks of fresh-baked brown bread. They dug in with a will.

After dinner, when Katya was tucked safely into bed and had fallen obligingly into a deep sleep—"Not to be heard from again until three A.M.," said her loving mother—the four of them gathered around the fireplace. Jim and Bobby drank coffee laced with Bobby's favorite Kentucky whiskey, and Dinah sat Kate down on a chair from the kitchen table, tucked a dishcloth around her neck, and proceeded to trim her hair.

"Is that normal behavior for posttraumatic stress syndrome, Bobby?" Kate asked him. "One minute, Riley Higgins was fine, conversing with me in a normal tone of voice. The next minute, he was screaming at the top of his lungs and hiding under the bed."

Bobby snorted. "There is no normal." He contemplated his mug and sighed. "You know one of the reasons I wound up in Alaska?"

"What?" Dinah bent Kate's head forward and to one side to trim the hair on the back of her neck. Snip, snip. Black hair whispered down to the cloth. Jim was mesmerized.

"Because," Bobby said, "Alaska was home to one of two—count 'em, only two—U.S. senators to vote against the Tonkin Gulf Resolution. Ernest Gruening, bless his bald head, whatever cloud he's sitting on, I hope he's got a babe on each arm and a gallon of sipping whiskey sitting in front of him that never goes dry." He raised his mug in a toast.

"I went over in '68, same year as Higgins. Jesus, what a year. Started off with Tet—welcome to Vietnam, and don't let the door hit you in the ass on your way out—Martin dead, Bobby dead, Chicago, the sit-ins, the riots, the demonstrations, Johnson quitting so he wouldn't have to lose a war, Nixon in—Jesus squared—man, everybody was just so pissed off at everybody else. There was no peace to be found anywhere in this country. And then—'one, two, three, what are we fightin' for'—off I go to the Vietnam War. Only, wait, it wasn't a war, because Congress never said it was, it was only a police action. And it sure as hell wasn't like the goddamn government had made any effort to convince me that I was fighting for truth, justice, and the American way."

He wheeled over to the stove and brought back the coffeepot, pouring warm-ups all around. Jim, still engrossed in

Kate's haircut, had to be nudged to get his attention. Miraculously, Bobby did not call it to everyone's attention at the top of his voice, for which Jim was profoundly thankful. "You know the difference between a war and a police action in the middle of the jungle, with the enemy planting mines and pongee sticks for you to walk on and your own zoomies hitting you with Agent Orange and napalm from overhead? I'll tell you. Nothing." He topped off his cup with the bottle of golden brown liquor that took pride of place on the end table next to the couch.

"Still," he said. "Sometimes we act like it's the only war that ever happened, that ever mattered. Shit. Some battles in the Civil War, they lost more casualties in a day than we lost in our whole time in the Nam."

"So you're not into self-pity," Jim said. How the hell long did it take to cut a head of hair, for God's sake? He shifted uncomfortably on the couch. "We got that. What about Higgins? What did his record say? Did something happen to him over there to make him like he is now?"

"Jesus H. Christ, haven't you been listening! Something happens to everybody over there, in every war!"

Katya, used to Daddy's bellow, slept serenely on, but Dinah gave him a severe look. More temperately, Bobby said, "Of course something fucking happened to him. He was stuck down in the middle of a jungle and people were shooting at him. Somebody shoved a rifle in his face and told him to shoot back. Maybe he shot a kid." He cast an involuntary glance over his shoulder at Katya. "Maybe he fragged his looie. Maybe his looie did a Calley and he went along, and maybe the only way he can deal with the world is not to come back to it. It happens. It happens in every war."

Bobby pointed with his mug. "And you have to consider this, too—maybe nothing happened. Maybe he was just one of those poor bastards who can't take combat, period. It was battle fatigue in World War Two, shell shock in World

War One, and they probably called it something else in the Civil War and something else again in the War of the Roses. Who the hell knows? Guys like Higgins, some can deal, some can't." He rubbed the stubs of the legs sticking out over the edge of his wheelchair. "Some can't," he repeated.

"He's crazy as a bedbug now," Jim said with a sigh. "I guess that's what matters." He looked back at Kate, and didn't know if he was relieved or disappointed to see Dinah untying the dishcloth and using it to flick hairs off Kate's shirt.

Kate was looking at Mutt, who was snoozing in front of the fireplace, her head resting on what looked like the jawbone of an ass, or maybe a woolly mammoth. "She let him scratch her head."

"What? Who?"

"Mutt. She let Higgins scratch her head."

Jim looked at Mutt. "You been stepping out on me, girl?"

Mutt twitched an ear but did not otherwise respond.

"The thing is," Kate said, and then thought better of it. "Never mind."

"Never mind what?"

Kate made a face. "She's good about people, okay? She doesn't like bad guys. And she let this guy scratch her head. It's just—odd, that's all." She looked sorry she'd said anything.

"Who wants dessert?" Dinah said briskly, folding the towel around the shears. "Apple pie, left over from the potlatch. Great potlatch, by the way, Kate. You done good."

"Yeah!" Bobby said. "That old broad would have had a hell of a good time. The true test of a good wake, if the deceased would have wanted to be there."

Dinah brought out pieces of pie adorned with whipped cream. It wasn't as good as Ruthe's rhubarb, but it wasn't bad.

"Listen, Bobby," Kate said, "did you ever hear anything

about Dina Willner being—ouch!" This when Jim kicked her, not gently, in the right shin. She glared. "What?"

"Great pie," Jim said, his mouth full. "Isn't it?"

Out on the porch, Jim said to Mutt, "So you let Higgins scratch your head, did you, girl?" He cast a look at Kate. "Considering the way she usually greets me, you must think I'm a prince."

"Why did you stop me from telling them about Dina and John Letourneau?"

"Because we're going to see Letourneau next, and I want to talk to him about it before Bobby broadcasts it on Park Air." He paused. "He wasn't at the potlatch."

"He doesn't go to them, usually. Why do you want to talk to him about it at all? It's ancient history. You said yourself that the marriage certificate was from twenty-five years ago. Jim!" She trailed after him to her snow machine, upon which she had found herself chauffeuring him around that afternoon. Mutt was lucky Kate had hooked up the trailer to bring the potlatch pictures into town. "And what's with this 'we?' "

"It's not that far. Stop whining and drive."

9

They trod the steps to the broad expanse of split-wood deck, neatly shoveled, a wrought-iron table leg peeping from beneath a lashed-down blue plastic tarp in one corner. She knocked, far too conscious of Jim Chopin standing directly behind her.

They waited. He must have heard them coming up the river road.

The door opened. "Hello, John," Jim said.

"Jim," John said. He looked down. "Kate. You're back. Come on in." He stepped back and pulled the door wide. "Get you a drink? Or some coffee?"

"Coffee'd be fine," Jim said.

John served it up in the same carafe on the same black lacquer tray, this time with a plate of Oreo cookies. "Got a sweet tooth," he explained, and took a handful for himself before he sat down. Mutt sat next to Kate's chair. She had not greeted Letourneau. He had not saluted her. "What can I do you for, Jim?"

"It's about Dina Willner."

Letourneau didn't start or pale. "That a fact. And why

would you think I would have anything to tell you about Dina Willner?"

Kate, watching Jim, saw the split second it took him to make up his mind. "Maybe because you were married to her."

"Mmm." Letourneau ate another cookie with studied nonchalance, but Kate, watching him now, got the impression that he was anything but unconcerned. "So we were. For about three seconds once, a long time ago."

"Twenty-five years ago, to be exact."

Letourneau's eyes moved restlessly beneath heavy lids. "If you say so."

"The marriage certificate at Dina's house says so."

"Ah. Surprised she kept that. Dina never was one to collect souvenirs."

"Tell me about it."

"No," Letourneau said coolly.

"No?" Jim said.

"No," Letourneau repeated, and stood up. "If that's all, I'll say good night."

"John." Jim sat where he was.

For the first time that evening, John Letourneau's voice rose. "I thought you had whoever killed her locked up in Tok."

"I thought I did."

Letourneau stiffened. "You thought you did? You mean you don't think he did it?"

"There are some loose ends."

There weren't, or not any that would stand up in court, Kate thought, and wondered again why she and Jim were there.

"Well, this isn't one of them. My marriage to Dina had nothing to do with her death."

"Why don't you tell me about it?" Jim wasn't the self-effacing type, but he could put on a pretty good show when he thought it might get him information he wouldn't get any other way.

The moment hung in the balance. It could have gone either way. Seconds ticked by.

Letourneau sighed and sat down again. Kate walked over and refilled her mug, grabbing up a couple of cookies while she was at it. She wandered over to the window and stared out on the moonlit expanse of river, frozen hard and, due to the stresses and strains exerted by the subsurface current, anything but smooth. It was covered with snow machine tracks, swooping and winding around bergs and pinnacles. An open lead streamed gently, then vanished as she watched, the ice closing it off again.

"What do you want to know?" Letourneau said. She turned to watch.

Now that he had what he wanted, Jim added a little humility for effect. "I don't know, John, I'm just fishing, really. It surprised me that Dina had been married."

Letourneau gave a short laugh. "It'd surprise a lot of people."

"I thought she came to the Park with Ruthe."

"She did."

"But . . ."

John's back was very straight. He seemed to Kate rather like a soldier marching into battle, facing heavy enemy fire yet determined to do his duty. "Back when I was just proving up on my homestead, back when Dina and Ruthe first bought the camp and started importing tourists, they got some who wanted to shoot with more than a camera. They farmed them out to me. They helped me get my start. I was ten years younger, but we had a lot in common, and there weren't a hell of a lot of other people around in those days. Dina and I got to know each other." He paused. "And then it got to be more than that."

"How did Ruthe feel about your relationship?"

"I don't know. I never talked to her about it."

"Come on, John."

"I don't know, damn it," Letourneau said sharply. "We eloped, just the two of us. Dina flew us to Ahtna. We got married by the magistrate there. We lasted a month."

"What happened?"

"It's personal."

"What happened?"

"I'm telling you it has nothing to do with Dina's death."

There was a time to ease up. This wasn't it. "What happened, John?"

Letourneau swore beneath his breath and got up to pace to the fireplace. It was the first time Kate had ever seen him lose his composure. He turned and gave them an angry look. "I took her away from Ruthe. Ruthe took her back. That's all I'm going to say about it."

There was present anger and remembered misery on John Letourneau's face. There was also the whip of humiliation, an emotion in a man of John Letourneau's age and upbringing that would matter more than the first two. He'd been outperformed by a lesbian. His woman had gone from him to another woman.

"And since?" Jim said.

Letourneau mastered his feelings and returned to his chair, making a business out of refilling his mug and biting into another cookie. "There is no since. We coexist. I even send customers their way. They do the same. We get along."

Kate remembered Dina tripping Letourneau with her cane on the Roadhouse dance floor ten days before. In Letourneauspeak, "get along" could mean anything short of murder.

Or it could mean murder.

It was a well-known maxim of law enforcement that the spouses of the unexpectedly deceased were always the prime suspects. *The nearest and the dearest got the motive with the mostest.* One of Jack Morgan's Laws.

But Jim Chopin had the prime suspect in custody. So what, Kate asked herself for the tenth time, were they doing here, exactly?

"You got along, did you?" Jim said.

Letourneau looked irritated. "What I said."

Jim pretended to consult a note on his pad. "That why you turned the Kanuyaq Land Trust into the IRS for using donations to politic instead of to buy land?"

What? Kate almost said, and then Jim caught her eye and she thought better of it.

Letourneau shrugged. "They were using money to lobby the legislature and Congress on environmental issues. Money raised specifically to underwrite land purchases in the Park. That's just wrong." He gazed at Jim benignly. "It was my public duty as a citizen to report that to the proper authorities."

Kate thought of what Dina's reaction would have been to that statement and now understood completely why they had come to John's lodge.

"I also heard the judge kicked the case," Jim said.

Letourneau shrugged again, and this time he smiled, too. He had regained his equilibrium. Kate had the uneasy and entirely unwarranted suspicion that it was because they had missed something, something he didn't want them to know, that he was glad that the conversation had turned into this channel, and that there were others they could have taken that would have been far more dangerous to him. "He disagreed with my attorneys. What can you do?"

"I also heard—"

"You hear a hell of a lot, now don't you?"

Unperturbed, Jim began again. "I also heard that you fought the increase in acreage to the wildlife refuge of the Park included in the d-2 lands bill."

"So? More wildlife refuge equals less hunting. I surely to heaven wasn't alone in that."

"Put you up against Dina and Ruthe."

"So did a lot of things. Nature of the businesses we were in, respectively."

Jim pondered for a moment. "Dina Willner thought enough of you at one time to marry you. Think she might have left you anything in her will?"

"What might that be," John Letourneau said very dryly, "maybe a half interest in Camp Teddy?" He laughed. "I guess you don't hear everything after all. Ruthe and Dina have joint rights of survivorship in Camp Teddy. When they're both dead, it goes to the Kanuyaq Land Trust."

"You've seen their wills?"

"No. Dina told me, back when we were married. Can't imagine they changed them. Now," John Letourneau said, rising to his feet and speaking with an air of finality, "I have told you more about my personal business than I have told anyone else, ever, and I still can see no way that it will help you convict someone already in custody. So I will say good night to you both."

As they left, Kate had the distinct impression that John Letourneau had learned more from them than they had from him. There was no reason for it to bother her, but it did.

They drove a mile without speaking. With Mutt crowded on behind, Jim's legs were so long that they wrapped around Kate's on either side. His hands rode lightly at her waist, his body a solid wall of warmth at her back. She was thinking more kindly of the cramped quarters of the Cessna when he raised his voice over the noise of the engine. "What wasn't he telling us?"

So Jim had picked up on that, too. She did him the courtesy of not pretending not to know what he was talking about. "Everybody has secrets, Jim."

"And usually they get to keep them," he said. "But not when it comes to murder. I'll find out. I always do."

The man they had left alone in the elaborate lodge came to the same conclusion. An hour later, he sat at an old Royal manual typewriter and pecked out a letter. He signed it, and reached for the shotgun leaning against the desk.

10

And we're here, why again?" Kate said. She knocked her boots free of snow at the door of the Park Service headquarters on the Step, at the same time moving just outside Jim's reach. "It's late and I'm tired, and you know perfectly well Dan O'Brian had nothing to do with Dina's death."

"I found him standing over the body," Jim countered. "He might have seen something, heard something. I have to talk to him."

"You already have."

He was silent for a moment. "Yeah."

Her gaze sharpened. "What?"

"I don't know." He shook his head. "A feeling, like maybe he's not telling me everything."

"Crap. Dan O'Brian's not a guy to withhold knowledge of a crime."

"Maybe," he said in a level voice. "Maybe not." He looked down at her and raised an eyebrow. "I told you I could have dropped you at Bobby's on the way."

Like she would have let him interrogate Dan O'Brian

without her being in the room. She stamped up the stairs without deigning to reply and then slammed into the building, nearly catching his nose in the door.

Well, at least she wasn't indifferent to his presence. He followed her down the hall, long legs eating up the distance between them.

Dan was still in his office, head down in a stack of paperwork. He looked up when they came in. "Great," he said, tossing down his pen. "Cheese it, it's the fuzz." Mutt trotted around the desk and bounced up for her usual exchange of sugar. "Except you, babe. You I'm happy to see anytime." He directed an unfriendly gaze at Jim. "What?"

Kate took up a strategic position perched on the corner of Dan's desk. Jim sat opposite and cocked one heel on the other corner, a relaxed pose that deceived no one. "Tell me again. Everything you saw, everything you heard, every detail—I don't care how insignificant you think it is."

"Jesus." Dan pushed away from the desk and leaned back, rubbing his face hard with both hands. "I've told you everything I know."

"Tell me again," Jim repeated.

Dan sighed sharply and dropped his hands to the desk in front of him. In a flat, dry voice, he repeated his story as if by rote. Due to Washington politics, his job was in jeopardy. He had consulted with friends (he didn't look at Kate) and had decided to fight for it, which meant asking Park rats with influence to intercede on his behalf. Dina Willner and Ruthe Bauman were wired into the conservation movement, his relationship with them was good, and so they were naturals to ask for help. He drove to their cabin. He found them—he swallowed. "I found them like that," he said. "Then I heard footsteps on the stairs, and I thought maybe this was who did it coming back." He rubbed his head, which still sported a knot on it, although reduced in size. "After that, it was like the Keystone Kops or something. I yanked the door open the same time somebody shoved it open from the outside, and bam! The next thing I know, I'm on the floor next to Dina, looking up at you coming through the door. I thought it was you who smacked me."

"It was Dandy, bringing the mail."

Dan nodded. "Yeah, he told me."

"What time was this?"

"Midafternoon. Say three, maybe? Three-thirty?"

"Did you see anything?"

"Other than stars? No."

"Hear anything?"

Dan sighed. "I wish. I didn't hear a damn thing."

Kate, watching, was alarmed to see that Jim's instincts had not deceived him. There was something that Dan wasn't saying. "Dan," she said.

"Goddamn it, Kate," he said, his voice rising. "Dina and Ruthe were and are friends of mine. Do you think if I knew something I wouldn't tell you? That I wouldn't want to help you find who did this horrible thing and kick the shit out of them myself?"

"No," Kate said, her voice by contrast calm, even soothing. "I don't think that."

And yet, as they walked down the path of hard-packed snow to where the snow machine sat waiting, she couldn't help thinking that Dan O'Brian had sounded as defensive as he had angry. He had wanted them out of his office, had seemed almost desperate to see them go. Here's your hat, what's your hurry. As if he had allowed them to stay, he might have said more than he wanted to.

Hearing Jim take a breath, she said, "Don't. Don't even go there."

She'd seen what he had, and that was all he'd been looking for. He exhaled without speaking. In grim silence, they mounted up, this time with Mutt, in response to a barked order, hopping between them.

Jim shifted on the couch in Bobby's living room, restless. It didn't help that he could hear the soft sound of Kate's regular breathing, and that his overactive imagination could put that sound much closer to him without any effort at all.

The fire crackled on the hearth. A log shifted and sparks flew upward, casting a faint glow over the dark head buried in the pillow on the other couch. It was a wide couch. Plenty of room. She probably wouldn't even wake up if he slid in next to her. She probably wouldn't even stir. Maybe she'd just roll over and he could curl into her spoon-fashion. He could slide his hands around her waist and pull her in tight. He thought of that ass against his crotch and had to shift again to make room for his erection. It didn't even bother him anymore; it was like the damn thing was on automatic around her.

He tried like hell not to think about it. Think about Riley Higgins instead, he told himself, and for a few moments he actually did. Bobby was right: The guy was a poor fucker, but that didn't in and of itself make Higgins not a murderer. Crazy people did crazy things. Higgins, by empirical evidence newly observed, was manifestly crazier than a bedbug. He could have taken out both Dina and Ruthe in one of his rages.

Kate stirred. He watched with hungry eyes as her body slid inside the sleeping bag. If he were lying beside her, he could slide his hands over her breasts. He tried to remember what they looked like, but everything had happened so fast that afternoon, he wasn't sure he'd even seen them. If he moved slowly enough, if he was smooth enough, maybe he'd get a look, before she ripped his balls off and Mutt ripped his throat out and Bobby shot him dead.

He rolled over and punched his pillow into a new shape. What about Dan O'Brian? What was going on there? He had worked cases with Dan O'Brian, he'd hoisted more than a few beers in his company, and he knew the man. Or thought he did. The last thing he wanted was to bring Dan O'Brian in and sweat him, but he was going to have to if Dan didn't open up. He didn't even want to think about the repercussions that would follow, both for Dan and for himself. He could just imagine what Billy Mike would have to say. And, oh god, Auntie Vi.

He didn't really think Mutt would rip his throat out. He wasn't 100 percent certain about Bobby. He was pretty sure Kate would rip his balls off, though.

Or not. She certainly had responded to him that afternoon at the cabin. No matter what she had said or done afterward, no matter how much she was avoiding the issue, no matter that she was twisting herself into a pretzel to deny the interlude, she had been with him all the way. He wondered how long it would take to get her back to that place.

On the plane back to Niniltna, he'd said, "So we're not going to talk about it?" Silence had been her answer. Okay, fine. He probably would want conversation somewhere down the line, but just at the moment, all he wanted was a month in bed, just the two of them, and the rest of the world held at bay with a big red KEEP OUT sign. Surely that wasn't too much to ask.

He wondered if, in the course of a normal sexual relationship, she was a talker or the quiet, intense type. The first time, she had called him Jack. The second time, she hadn't said anything at all. Of course, he had not been spectacularly articulate himself.

He wondered what her favorite position was. He'd had some imaginative partners in his life. But face it, Chopin, he told himself. If acquiring Kate Shugak as a partner means the missionary position for the foreseeable future, you'll take it and love it.

He wondered how long and what it took to make her come. He wondered if she screamed when she did. Well, he kind of knew the answers to both those questions now.

He stifled a groan and rolled over on his back.

He wondered if he was ever going to get laid again in his lifetime.

Why her? he asked himself for what might have been the thousandth time. Why this one stubborn, independent, irritating, exasperating woman? She was certainly far too short, especially for him. They'd look like Mutt and Jeff. Where had all the tall blondes in his life suddenly gone? The tall, charming, amenable, accommodating blondes, the ones who were waiting for him when he got to their houses and who let him go again without question the morning after?

The ones who cared as much for him as he did for them.

He remembered again that day in September when he and George had flown into George's hunting lodge south of Denali and had found Kate Shugak, covered in blood and dirt, keening a dirge to the lifeless body of her lover clasped in her arms. No one had ever loved him that much.

Tell the truth, Chopin, he thought. You never knew it was possible until you saw Kate with Jack. You thought it was something you read in a book or saw at the movies. You never thought it could happen in real life.

He kicked free of the sleeping bag, feeling through his T-shirt the heat of the wood burning in the fireplace.

He was, he realized, circling perilously close to the *L* word. He'd stared down men with .357s with less fear. He thought of his parents, those two strangers in the split-level house in San Jose, one staring at the television, the other logged onto the Internet, looking for the next cruise they could take. They had been married for forty years, and he couldn't remember an outward sign of affection more passionate than a chaste kiss, usually on the cheek. He supposed they loved each other, but he had long since decided that if that was love, no thank you. If he'd caught them groping each other in the kitchen, just once, maybe he

would have looked at life and relationships a little differently. He didn't know.

He didn't know a goddamned thing.

Kate shifted and murmured something.

Except that he had a ferocious and apparently perpetual
itch that it seemed only this woman could scratch. He raised
his head. "Kate?" he said softly. "You awake?"

"No, she isn't awake, you moron," Bobby's voice hissed
from the far corner, "and if you don't fucking shut up and
settle down, I'm going to toss you outside on your goddamn ear."

It was a long night.

He was shoveling in Dinah's ambrosial French toast and
Bobby's caribou sausage links the next morning about nine
o'clock when Dandy Mike came rushing up the steps.

Jim hung his head over his plate, wishing Dandy away.
"No," he said.

It didn't work. "Jim!" Dandy said. "You've got to
come!"

"Haven't we done this before?" Jim wondered out loud.

"You have to come! John Letourneau is dead!"

There was an electric moment. Jim's eyes met Kate's. "I
beg your pardon?"

"John Letourneau is dead!" Dandy said again, impatient.
"Come on, you have to come!"

Jim, still holding Kate's gaze—did she look as heavy-eyed
as he felt, or was it just his imagination?—said, "John Letourneau is dead? Where?"

"At his house," Dandy said, calmer now. "I went over to
borrow his grill for a party I'm throwing this afternoon, and
when he didn't answer the door, I went around the back
to find the grill, and I saw him through the window."

"You're sure he's dead?"

Dandy flushed. "Yes. I checked this time. His heart's not beating and he's cold."

"Anybody with you when you went?"

"Scottie Totemoff." Naturally. Scottie Totemoff was Dandy Mike's boon companion. He wondered how Demetri and Billy, both hardworking, responsible men, good providers, good husbands, good fathers, had managed to produce two of the biggest layabouts the Park had ever seen. "He was going to help me with the grill. And the party."

"Of course he was," Jim murmured. Undoubtedly, and the drinking.

"I left Scottie to keep watch, make sure nobody gets in to contaminate the scene." He waited to see the effect caused by this mastery of the language of his newly adopted profession.

"There's no hurry, then," Jim said mildly, and drank his coffee. "I might as well finish my breakfast."

Scottie was waiting for them on the deck, pacing back and forth. "About time you got here," he told Dandy. "I'm freezing my ass off."

"Why didn't you go inside?"

"There's a dead guy inside!"

"You'll have to get used to that if you want to work with us," Dandy said importantly. "Right, Jim?"

"What?" Kate said.

"Let's take a look," Jim said, and went inside.

John had been hurled backward out of his chair by the force of the blast, which had sheered off the left side of his chest. The room was spattered with most of it. Dandy's tracks between door and body were very clear.

The shotgun had fallen with him. His finger was still hooked inside the trigger guard.

"Didn't put it in his mouth," Jim said.

"Sometimes they don't," Kate said. "Usually it's because they don't want to mess up their faces."

"John probably didn't want to mess up his hair," said Jim. Kate looked at him. "Sorry. Cop humor."

She pointed. "He left a note."

"I see it." It stuck out of the old typewriter like a banner. Jim bent over to read it. " 'I killed Dina Willner. I'm too old to go to jail.' "

"Wait a minute." Kate stepped up to peer around him. "That's it? What the hell kind of suicide note is that? He doesn't say why?"

"He doesn't even say how." Jim stood up. "So, okay. This totally sucks."

In Kate's opinion, it could not have been better put, even if it would have sounded more appropriate coming out of Johnny's mouth.

Rigor was well established and Letourneau was difficult to move. Getting him into the back of Dandy's truck was bad enough, but Jim thought he was going to have to break one of Letourneau's legs to get the body into the Cessna. He was inexpressibly relieved when he didn't.

After forming an honor guard escort to the airport, Dandy and Scottie had peeled off to the Roadhouse, where, in spite of sworn promises to the contrary, he knew they were fast spreading the word. "I'll fly him into Ahtna," Jim said to Kate. "Get the body off to the lab."

"Do you doubt that it was suicide?"

Jim shook his head. "I doubt big time that he killed Dina Willner and assaulted Ruthe Bauman. I don't doubt that he killed himself." He thought about it. "Was he sick, do you know?"

"What, you mean like crazy?" Kate snorted. "Like a fox. John Letourneau was one of the saner men I've ever met."

"I don't mean like crazy, I mean like cancer, something like that."

"Not that I know of."

"Was he broke?"

"Not that I know of. Park rats say John's got the first dime he ever made."

Jim shook his head. "Then I don't get it. What makes a man confess to a murder he didn't commit and then kill himself?"

There was a short silence. "He wanted us to stop looking," Kate said slowly.

"Bingo. I'm really thinking Riley didn't do it now, Kate. But I'm going to need a shitload of proof, and I'm going to need it fast."

Kate turned to him. "From the state of the rigor, I'd say he did it not very long after we left."

"Less than an hour would be my guess," Jim said.

Kate nodded. "Me, too. What did we say to trigger this?"

He said quickly, "It doesn't have to be us. He could have made up his mind to do it before we got there. We could have held him up."

She flapped an irritated hand. "Calm down. I don't feel responsible." He looked at her. "I don't, Jim," she said in a quiet voice, her eyes meeting his without reservation.

It was probably the most open look she'd given him since the other afternoon, and it encouraged him to say rashly, "Kate. We need to talk."

She stiffened. "No, we don't."

"Yeah. We do. And we will." He looked at the body in the back of the plane, up at the falling snow, and repressed an oath. "But not now. Soon, though."

She opened her mouth, then closed it again. He thought she sighed. Goaded, he said, "I know you want me."

"I'm not a child with her face pressed up to the candy store window," she said. "I don't let myself have everything I want."

His smile flashed out. "I like it that you compare me to candy."

The smile, with its manifest, practiced charm, was enough

by itself to make her angry all over again. She was relieved. For a moment, she'd been afraid that she could no longer be angry with him. It helped her say firmly, "Too much candy makes me sick to my stomach."

It sounded prissy even to her own ears. He laughed, a spontaneous baritone sound that rang out down the strip like someone was tolling a bell, and she wanted to kill him.

He took off, the Cessna disappearing into the low overcast almost immediately. The weather was purportedly better in Ahtna, but if the ceiling came down any lower, he'd be unable to return to Niniltna today. She stood there, watching him go, a scowl on her face, trying to make up her mind if that was a good thing or a bad thing. "Hell with it," she said, and kicked a chunk of ice out of her path on the way back to her snow machine. Mutt sensed her roommate's uncertain temper and maintained a discreet silence.

Kate killed the engine of the snow machine in front of John Letourneau's front steps, still scowling. She didn't know why she was back here, nor did she know what she was looking for that Jim wouldn't already have found. Mutt, sitting next to her, whined an inquiry. "Beats the hell out of me," she said.

They went inside. Kate found John's bedroom and a hamper containing dirty clothes. She held a sock out to Mutt, who sniffed it with interest and looked up, brows raised. "Anybody else been here?" Mutt sneezed once to clear her head and started nosing around the room.

They found nothing out of the ordinary in John's bedroom. The guest bedrooms, running along both sides of the lodge on the second floor, had been scrubbed clean after the last client had flown south for the winter. They proved equally uninteresting. The kitchen was spotless, and none of the three tables in the dining room looked like they had been used in the last few months. The living room didn't look as if it saw regular use, either. If you discounted the blood and bits of flesh, bone, and organ drying hard to floor, wall, and window, the office was neat, well organized, and up-to-date, nothing in the in basket, the files in the metal cabinet meticulously alphabetized in drawers marked CLIENTS, SUPPLIERS, EMPLOYEES, and TAXES.

The whole place was as neat as a hospital that never admitted any patients.

"Where did this guy live?" Kate wondered out loud as she opened the door off the living room.

Ah.

It was a smaller room than the vast expanses to be found elsewhere in this mausoleum, and made smaller by the amount of stuff crowded into it. A bookcase took up one entire wall, containing the *Gun Digest,* the *Shooter's Bible, Black's Wing and Clay, Black's Fly Fishing, The Milepost,* the *Alaska Almanac,* and everything Boone and Crockett had ever published, from *B&C Big Game Awards* for the previous twenty years to *Spirit of Wilderness,* essays in eight editions appearing to have been written by such low-key guest authors as Theodore Roosevelt and Norman Schwarzkopf. One whole shelf was dedicated to maps of Alaska and the Park, starting with the *Alaska Atlas & Gazetteer* and ending with the USGS survey of the Park, commissioned after d-2 to illustrate the new boundaries. That survey in hand, along with a compass, Kate could walk from Ahtna to Cordova and never get her feet wet.

There were no trophies on the walls of this room. There was a mahogany-stained gun case. It was locked, but Kate could see two empty cradles through the glass pane on the door, and four other cradles filled with serviceable but not particularly exciting weapons, none of them new, none of them elaborately chased with silver scrollwork, none of them with carved walnut stocks. Three of them didn't even have scope mounts. Evidently, John wasn't into collecting. There was a drawer at the base of the cabinet, unlocked, containing boxes of ammunition.

There was one chair, a dark brown leather recliner, a floor lamp next to it. Stacked on the end table, within reach, were copies of *Field & Stream*, *Fair Chase*, and *Alaska Magazine*, dog-eared where his own ad appeared.

The ad took up a quarter of a page and was simple and direct: "We offer the world's best hunting and fishing, with experienced guides, no crowds, deluxe accommodations and gourmet meals." There was a picture of a big bull moose with a magnificent rack standing knee-deep in a tiny lake, with the Quilaks rearing up stunningly in the background. An 800 phone number appeared at the moose's feet.

Apparently, John had not been a proponent of the hard sell. As many years as he had in his business, he probably got most of his clients by word of mouth and repeat business.

There was a television and a VCR in a cabinet opposite the recliner. The shelf below the VCR was packed with tapes bearing titles like *Ecstasy* and *Exposed* and *Insatiable*. A do-it-yourselfer, John Letourneau. It was an effective means of soothing the savage, but lonesome. Resolutely, Kate turned her mind from thoughts of her and Jim on the floor of the mountain cabin.

She wandered back out into the living room to stare through the window at the river. This was a lonely place, or it felt like it to Kate. But really, what was loneliness anyway? She was alone a lot of the time, she was used to it, she liked it, and she was good at it. She preferred autonomy to dependence. At the homestead, she had books to read and music to listen to, bread to bake and snow to shovel, fish to pick and traps to check, a rifle to clean and moose to hunt, butcher, and pack. People seldom knocked at her door. Her nearest neighbor was, at any given time, a bull moose or a grizzly sow or the big bad gray wolf that kept trying to seduce Mutt into forsaking Kate and civilization for him and the call of the wild.

The great thing about the moose and the grizzly and the wolf was that they had not been gifted by their creator with the power of speech. They couldn't make conversation. The moose might kick your ass and the grizzly might rip it off and the wolf might eat it, but they wouldn't talk you to death while they got on with the job.

The main thing Kate had against people was that they talked too much and said too little.

She wondered now if she and John Letourneau had had that much in common.

She also wondered how much she and Jim Chopin had in common. Once upon a time, the immediate answer would have been a loud, definite "Nothing!" but Kate Shugak wasn't into lying, not even to herself, and it was more than time that she took a good long look at this fatal attraction she seemed to be developing. Feeling panic close up the back of her throat, she beat it back and tried talking herself down.

For starters, Jim Chopin was nothing at all, in no respect, like Jack Morgan.

Except that he was tall. And in law enforcement. And had a deep voice. And was good at his job.

And was, she knew now, just as capable of firing her engine on all eight cylinders without taking his boots off. God. She closed her eyes and for a weak moment gave into memory. It had been like tigers mating, all teeth and claws. Who would have thought Jim Chopin, the man who raised self-discipline to a whole new level, could go that wild?

And just what was that, that little feeling buried away in the back of her mind where she couldn't get at it? That couldn't be pride, could it? That she had done that to him, had caused him to lose control so completely, had shown him just how thin the veneer of civilization lay upon him?

Starting to get that panicky feeling again, she seized upon the indisputable fact that Jim was a rounder with positive relief. She was a one-man woman. He was a many-womaned man. Ergo, it would be very, very bad for her to enter into any kind of relationship with him. Maybe it was just pride, she didn't like looking down the road and seeing herself as one in a long line of Chopper Jim's ex-girlfriends, littering the Park from the Brooks Range to the Gulf of Alaska. So? Pride wasn't necessarily a bad thing.

Neither was self-preservation. Maybe she was afraid that any relationship they developed would mean more to her than it would to him. Maybe she was afraid that down the road she would be dumped, good and hard.

She gave herself an annoyed shake. "I'm not afraid," she told the view. "It's not that at all."

The view remained serenely uncommunicative.

"Damn you, Jack!" she yelled. "Why'd you have to go and leave me here all alone?"

The words reverberated off glass and wood and rang in her ears. She closed her eyes against the sound and stood where she was, fists shoved into her pockets, rage and fear waging a battle for preeminence inside her.

Mutt's claws ticky-tacked across the wood floor. She paused next to Kate, who opened her eyes, took a deep, shaky sigh, and looked down, to see Mutt deposit a white knit hat on the floor at her feet.

"What's this?" Kate bent to pick it up.

It was a standard knit hat, a ribbed tube of two-ply white yarn pulled tight and tied off at one end and turned up into a brim at the other. Kate touched it experimentally. It was very soft, and fuzzy. Kate had a very faint acquaintance with yarn, as the four aunties were always either quilting or knitting. This might be angora, or have some angora in it. It wasn't synthetic; it didn't have that snag on her calluses.

She sniffed it. There was a faint flowery smell. She examined the inside of the brim and found a fair hair that was either pale blond or white.

She tried to imagine the hat on John Letourneau's head and failed. "Where did you find it, girl? Show me."

Mutt led her to the door. There was a bench next to it with a lid. Mutt nosed open the lid, and Kate saw that the compartment held a selection of hats, gloves, and scarves, some leather, some knit, some felt.

There were no matching gloves or scarf for the hat, but then, nothing in the bench matched anything else. They were all probably spares, some John had bought, some clients had left behind, available for future guests with chills. And probably each and every one had a different smell to it. Mutt gave her a pitiful look. "Not your fault, girl." Kate tossed the hat back inside and closed the lid.

John Letourneau's suicide might just be one of those little mysteries of life that remained unsolved. It comforted Kate, at least a little, to know they still existed. Unlike Jim Chopin, she didn't want everything to be neatly explained, all the loose ends tied up and tucked away. She liked to think she'd leave a mystery or two behind herself. Just not anytime soon.

"Come on," she said to Mutt. "Let's go say hi to Bernie."

11

The Roadhouse was packed to the rafters that afternoon. Dan O'Brian was at the bar, sitting as close as he could get to the serving station. Christie was all business, bestowing a smile on him in passing, the same smile she gave Kate on her way to a table, a loaded tray balanced on her right hand. The table the tray was headed for, Kate was interested to note, contained among its patrons one Pete Heiman. His face lit up as Christie approached, and her hand settled onto his shoulder in what seemed to Kate to be a very comfortable gesture.

Kate let Mutt lead the way to a seat next to Dan, who said, "What's this I hear about John Letourneau?"

"Only the truth, I'm sure," Kate said, looking over her shoulder at the table where Dandy and Scottie were holding forth before an admiring crowd, most of them women. For a place where the ratio of men to women was five to one, Dandy Mike got more than his share.

Christie arrived at Dandy's table with refills, and he smiled up at her, resting a familiar hand a little too low on her waist. She smiled down at him and shifted out of reach. Kate heard Dan sigh.

She looked at him and he grinned, although the expression held more than a little constraint. They were both remembering the interview in his office.

"Hey, Kate," Bernie said, sliding a glass in front of her that proved to hold Diet 7Up.

"Bernie," she said, "can I have some water?"

He cocked an eyebrow. "No profit in that."

"Club soda, then. With lime. I'll pay for the lime."

"Sure, but you're kinda breaking my streak, Kate," he said, and tossed a piece of beef jerky to the large grayears standing at attention next to Kate. A low "Woof!" and the ears disappeared.

Auntie Vi was there with one of her sons. Kate squinted through the dim light. Roger, she thought. Roger's wife was there, too, and three of their four children. Mary Balashoff was visiting from Alaganik—Mary must have given up on prying Old Sam loose from the Park—and she and Old Sam were pegging like mad in a fierce game of cribbage. The four Grosdidiers had commandeered their usual table with the ringside seat in front of the television set hanging from one corner of the room, groaning at a bad call by the referee of the football play-off game presently on the screen.

The door opened and Jim Chopin stepped inside. There was the usual lull when five-foot twenty-two inches of state trooper blue and gold stepped majestically into the room, but when it became apparent he wasn't there to arrest anyone, the noise soon regained its proper level and he was allowed to walk to the bar unmolested.

"Kate," he said.

Kate was aware that Dan had braced himself on the stool next to her. "You made it back."

"It stayed above minimums. Barely." He pulled off the ball cap with the trooper emblem on the front and ran his hand through his hair, which looked a little less immaculate than usual. "Bernie."

"Jim. Can't beat you off with a stick lately." Jim didn't offer an explanation for his presence that evening, and with the delicate tact required of the professional bartender, Bernie didn't ask. Besides, he had a pretty fair idea that he already knew. "What'll you have?"

Jim never drank on duty. It was an obligation he felt he owed the uniform, but it had been a long day and he would have killed for a long cold one. "Coke," he said finally, and sighed when he said it.

"You get out all right?" Kate said.

"Yeah. I missed the last plane into Anchorage, but Kenny Hazen put the body in the local meat locker and promised to get it on the first plane tomorrow." His Coke arrived and he looked at it sadly. "Not that an autopsy is going to tell us anything we don't already know." He allowed himself to take notice of Dan O'Brian. "Hey, Dan."

Dan shifted on his stool. "Hey, Jim."

A brief silence ensued.

"I went back out to the lodge," Kate said.

Jim looked at her, his eyes sharpening. "Why?"

"Because. I'm like you—I can't figure out why he did it. I looked through his papers, Jim. If he was dying of disease, he didn't know it. He had money in the bank; all his bills were paid, all his workman's comp up-to-date. He'd sent his chef and some of the long-term employees Christmas bonuses, the rest of them Harry and David fruit boxes. There's just no reason for what he did."

"Maybe he was lonely," Dan said, who had been listening and looked relieved, probably because the conversation had taken a turn away from him.

Lonely. There was that word again. Kate set her teeth and drank club soda. She wondered what a shot of scotch, neat, would do to firm up her backbone, and was immediately appalled that such a thought would come within thinking distance of her teetotaling brain. Just another example of how keeping bad company can decay your moral fiber, she told herself.

Jim saw her stiffen and wondered who'd shoved what poker up her spine. Lucky for him that he wasn't interested in easy. He wished he could have a beer. He wished he could have several. He wished he could take Kate Shugak to bed and not leave it for the foreseeable future.

Christie, taking a break, was standing next to Dan, who had his arm around her. Her bright blue eyes were watching as she listened. "Maybe Mr. Letourneau was just tired."

"He didn't have any business being tired," Kate said crossly. "He was only sixty something. For a Park rat, that's practically the prime of life. At sixty Park rats are just getting started. They quit jobs and go back to school, they go into business, they get married and start family, they—"

Dan snorted. "Right. John Letourneau, married, with children. That would have happened."

Jim said to Kate in a quiet voice, "What?"

She stared at their reflection in the mirror at the back of the bar. "I just thought—"

"What did you just think?"

"I—nothing." She shook her head. "No. Nothing."

"You sure?" Their eyes met in the mirror. "You looked like you were having an epiphany there for a second."

She smiled, a little rueful, but her smiles were rare in his direction and he'd take what he could get. "A crazy idea, nothing worth saying out loud." She raised her glass and drank. "So, Christie, how are you liking the Park?"

Christie gave Dan a long, sultry look. "I'm liking what I've found here."

Dan actually quivered all over. With difficulty, Kate refrained from rolling her eyes. Kick me, hit me, beat me; I'll love you anyway and maybe even because of it. What was it with guys and the stick-and-carrot treatment? Christie had been all over Pete Heiman at the potlatch, and the Bush who were always looking for something to borrow. Certainly he had none who were invited to stay for free.

The lodge had all the echoing charm of an airport waiting lounge. The cabin was dusty and cluttered and crowded to the point that you couldn't take a step without knocking over a stack of magazines, but it was a lot friendlier than the lodge. If the building was a reflection of the man, Kate could well understand the qualities Dina had found lacking in John.

Kate had overheard a conversation when she was younger that made her aware that Dina and Ruthe were a couple, a pair, like husband and wife, only not. It was a thing she'd never heard of, a woman and a woman, and by that time, she knew her own predilection was strictly men, so it was hard for her to comprehend.

On the other hand, their relationship wasn't hard for her to accept. They were still Dina and Ruthe, her grandmother's friends, and hers. Ruthe was a great cook and Dina could outhike anything on two legs or four, and both of them could fly anything with wings. They were smart and they told funny stories, and when anyone in the Park needed help, they were there. She didn't need to know anything about their sleeping arrangements to know that they were some of the best neighbors the Park had. Long winters made for intimate relationships over distances that would be unthinkable in a city suburb. Good neighbors were crucial.

Once Jack had come into Kate's life, she had never looked at another man. Well. Before Dinah came on the scene, there had been that brief, intense interval with Bobby Clark, and then there was Ken Dahl, poor dead bastard. And if she were being completely honest, there had been one or two tense moments with Jim Chopin.

Maybe more than one or two. And maybe more than moments. And maybe one of them right here.

But that isn't the point, she thought, rousing herself. The point was she couldn't account for Dina's sudden, brief

telegraph being what it was, Kate couldn't believe Dan hadn't heard about it. What did Dan think all that action over at Dandy's and Pete's tables was about? Men. Were they blind, or was it just that they couldn't see?

Whatever. It wasn't any of her business, thank god. Kate got a refill and enticed Bernie into a long, detailed discussion on the possibilities of Niniltna bringing home the state's Class C men's varsity basketball championship. Seldovia was this year's favorite, with Chuathbaluk a close second, but Bernie was confident his team would pull it out.

Basketball, now there was a game men could play.

And ought to stick to.

When she left the Roadhouse an hour later, the sun had set behind the clouds and it was beginning to snow again, the remnants of the storm that had been coming off the Gulf in fits and starts since the day after they had found Dina and Ruthe.

Kate loved falling snow. She loved the look of it, light, powdery flakes that seemed to vanish as they floated gracefully to the ground. She loved the feel of it, the wet, cool shock as it touched the skin of her upturned face. She loved the way it seemed to displace sound. No airplane ever seemed so loud in the falling snow, no boat, truck, or snow machine. Falling snow toned a shout down to a murmur and then absorbed the murmur, imposing its own sweet, silent hush on a noisy world.

She stood motionless next to the snow machine, her face turned to the sky, until Mutt nudged her hand in a purposeful manner. She sighed and mounted. Mutt leapt up behind her and gave her an encouraging look. "You have no soul," Kate told her as she started the engine.

Jim was going to rent one of Bernie's cabins for the night. Kate had given it some thought but then decided to head back to Bobby's, snow or no snow. Not that she didn't trust herself, but she'd feel better with twenty-seven miles between her and the trooper.

There wasn't much traffic—a couple of other snow machines and a dogsled going in the other direction, but the rest of the road was theirs. Snowflakes made white streaks in the headlights. A pair of eyes flashed out at them from beneath the heavily frosted skirts of a spruce tree. An arctic hare bounded across the road, giving Kate just enough time to let up on the gas without sending Mutt over her shoulder and jackknifing the trailer.

They came to a stop just a few feet short of the turnoff to Camp Teddy.

She meditated for a few moments, looking at the narrow trail that snaked up the hill to Dina and Ruthe's aerie. "We'll just be a few minutes," she said to Mutt.

Mutt gave the impression that she was prepared to put up with the detour, for a price to be negotiated later.

It amazed her how normal the inside of the cabin looked. There ought at least to be the scorched outline of two bodies beneath the coffee table.

"Knock it off, Shugak," she said to herself sternly, and then was embarrassed when Mutt gave her a quizzical look. "I talk to you, don't I?" she asked her.

Mutt gave her a long, assessing look, beneath which Kate tried not to squirm, and went to stand in front of the door. "Fine," Kate said. "Go chase birds. Leave me all alone here, talking to my ghosts."

Mutt did. No dependence could be placed on laying a guilt trip on a dog that was mostly wolf. Kate shut the door firmly behind her, not really trying to catch the tip of Mutt's tail in the door, but not trying really hard not to, either.

She leaned on the door handle and surveyed the cabin. At least it didn't look as if anyone else had shown up to appropriate whatever was lying around. She'd made sure

that Bernie spread the word that the cabin was under her protection, but all the same, she thought she had a padlock and a hasp rattling around the garage at home that she might fit to the front door, and maybe a bolt for the back door, as well. There had been a time when the cabin could have stood empty for weeks, months, maybe even years without suffering any harm. She hoped that time was still here, but she no longer had as much faith in the notion that she had once had.

Kate started a fire in the woodstove and brewed a cup of tea on the gas hot plate, added honey, and, not without some qualms, sat down in Dina's chair.

She had never looked at the cabin from this angle before. Dina's chair sat to the left of the woodstove and faced the northeast corner of the cabin. It was a great location from which to view the titles of the books on the shelves. The stove sat in the middle of the room, its exposed stovepipe chimney going straight up to the ceiling, which acted as a great heat radiator and provided a central location around which the furniture and fixtures would be arranged. Still, it seemed odd to Kate that with two enormous picture windows that took up practically the whole south wall of the cabin, the chairs Dina and Ruthe sat in most often faced in the opposite direction. Kate would have taken advantage of the view.

Although there would be more privacy at the back of the cabin, if you had guests who used the deck outside to look at the view, too. Kate put up the footrest and cupped the mug in her hands.

She compared John Letourneau's enormous, barely lived in lodge to this cabin. Here, there was just enough room for Dina and Ruthe. When friends came to stay, they were put up in one of the cabins on the hill. The paying guests took their meals in the mess hall above the cabins; the friends dined with Dina and Ruthe below. John, so far as Kate knew, had had no visitors, other than guys like Dandy

marriage to John Letourneau. Chemistry? Propinquity? Dina deciding later in life to conform to the straight and narrow?

None of it seemed very likely. Nor was Kate ever apt to come up with a better answer, unless Ruthe woke up and knew it.

The little gray lockbox was sitting on one of the bookshelves. She got it and sat back down.

There was the marriage certificate, a few simple lines, Dina and John's names, the date. Dina had been forty-five, John thirty-five.

Like John, Kate wondered why Dina had kept the certificate. A memento of one good month? A reminder of a lesson well learned?

She looked through the rest of the paperwork. A Social Security card. Two passports, both long out-of-date, although they had been well used in their time, from all over Europe to the Far East. A copy of the deed to the property of Camp Theodore. Two wills, in separate sealed envelopes, marked WILL on the outsides, "To Be Opened in the Event Of" in smaller writing below.

She opened Dina's. It was a copy. It was also very short. Dina hadn't owned a lot. Her interest in the camp went to Ruthe, unless Ruthe predeceased her, in which case it went into the Kanuyaq Land Trust, to be administered by the chief ranger of the Park and utilized as part of the national park as he or she saw fit. She directed that all of her possessions be sold, the proceeds also to go to the Kanuyaq Land Trust, with a few exceptions, noted in the attached list, items that she directed her executor to distribute.

Kate turned the page. The books went to Ruthe. There was some jewelry in a safety-deposit box in Anchorage, also bequeathed to Ruthe.

A note, added by hand and dated just this past November, said, "To Johnny Morgan, my photograph album, in the hope that he will continue to learn and grow."

Kate had to blink away sudden tears. She was about to put the will back in the envelope, when a phrase caught her eye. "I declare that, except as otherwise provided for in this Will, I have intentionally and with full knowledge omitted to provide for any heirs of mine who may be living at the date of my death, and I direct that such persons, if any, shall take no part of my estate."

Lawyers. Kate shook her head. Dina's parents had died in an accident before World War II, and she had had no children of her own. If she and John had stayed married a little longer, it might have been a different story.

"Oh," Kate said. She remembered now what she had thought of at the Roadhouse. Suddenly, it didn't seem so silly.

At that moment, she realized that it might not have been such a good idea to have spoken so freely of John Letourneau while standing in the Roadhouse with god and everybody else listening in.

Perhaps she should have stayed in one of the cabins, within earshot of a big, strong state trooper who had within reach a great big gun.

The door opened. She knew who it was without turning around, but she turned around anyway.

Christie Turner stood in the doorway, rifle in hand.

Kate got to her feet, careful to make no sudden movement. "You're John and Dina's daughter," she said.

Christie smiled. "So you figured it out, did you? I thought you might." She stepped inside, leaving the door open behind her.

"You don't seem too upset about it."

Christie pushed her hood back. "I've heard a lot of stories about you since coming into the Park. As soon as I saw you with the trooper, I knew there might be trouble." She smiled again. Her beautiful blue eyes held an expression that made the hair rise on the back of Kate's neck. Where was Mutt? Please let her stay away, Kate thought, please, please, please.

"You killed Dina," Kate said.

"Ah, my dear mother," Christie said. She gave the cabin a critical look. "Imagine, choosing this over the place my loving father built for her. She really wasn't worthy of me."

"Why?" Kate said.

"Why?" Christie wasn't as calm as she pretended to be. "Why? Oh, well, maybe because my loving mother gave me up for adoption to a couple of people who weren't fit to raise a cockroach. Tell me, Kate, were you fucked at four?"

"Depends on what you mean by fucked," Kate said.

Christie's eyes narrowed. "Fucked, as in screwed, as in raped, a big fat cock in and up every possible orifice." Her voice rose. "That's what I mean by *fucked*!"

"Then no," Kate said.

Christie reined in her fury. Her self-control was more frightening to Kate than a screaming fit would have been. "Of course you weren't. You fight on the side of the down-trodden and the oppressed. God help anyone if they mistreat a child in your presence. You'd mount up and ride to the rescue in a heartbeat. That's what you're all about. Truth, justice, and the American way."

It was an eerie echo of Bobby's comment about the Vietnam War. "You sound like you're pissed I wasn't there."

Christie laughed without humor. "Oh, you were there all right. You were there times ten, times twenty. All the lovely little policemen, and social workers, and lawyers, and judges. All of them so determined to do the right thing. All of them so totally without a clue." Her seraphic blue eyes stared over Kate's shoulder, unblinking, into the past. They held a blank, queer expression that was oddly familiar to Kate. She couldn't identify it, and then she could. Riley Higgins had had that same mad look in his eye just before he had dived beneath his bunk.

He hadn't held a rifle, though. "Yeah, yeah, yeah," Kate said.

The blue eyes came back to her face, narrowing now.

"Heard all this crap before," Kate said, and faked an elaborate yawn. There was no place to retreat, so attack was the only option. "It's always god or somebody else's fault with you people."

Christie's eyes narrowed in fury. " 'You people'?"

Good, Kate thought, get good and mad. She edged forward an inch, then another, unnoticed. "Yeah, you people who have to blame everything bad that happens in your lives on somebody else. The jails are full of you."

Christie gripped the rifle. "I was four years old!"

"I heard." Kate did her best to sound bored. "You can only blame so much on the way you were raised. Sooner or later, you have to start taking some responsibility for your own life."

"What do you call this?" Christie worked the bolt on the rifle and peered into the chamber.

Kate could see the brass gleaming from where she stood. "So you take out your birth mother for something that happened to you that she didn't even know about? Why didn't you start with your adoptive mother?"

Christie's smile was sly. "Who says I didn't?"

Jesus. Kate measured the distance between them. Still too far for her to take Christie down before Christie could bring up the rifle. Plus, there was too much furniture in the way. Contrary to what appeared to be popular opinion, Kate did not leap tall buildings in a single bound. "How?" Kate said. "How did you get here? There weren't any tracks. Jim looked. So did I."

"Same way I got here tonight," Christie said. Her smile was smug. "Cross-country."

Kate remembered something Dan had said. "Skis," she said.

"I waited until snow was forecast, and then I came and I killed them both." She laughed, an excited, high-pitched giggle that was too much like the laugh Kate had heard in the bar. Like, and different. "Bernie knows I like to take my break outside, and the snow here is terrific. With the right wax, I can do four miles in twenty minutes. It didn't even take the whole lunch hour."

"And John?"

Christie shrugged. "Ah, yes, dear old Dad." Her smile was sharp. "He wanted me to move in with him. Can you believe that? I never got so much as a goddamn birthday card from him, ever, and it was a little too late for him to start playing father." Her smile was quicksilver and malicious. "Besides, I already know how to play daddy. I had a wonderful teacher."

"He didn't even know you existed," Kate said.

"He should have!" Christie shouted. "He should have," she said again, more quietly this time.

"What are you going to do now?"

"Well." Christie thought about it. "You're the only one who knows. I guess I'll have to kill you." She smiled again.

Kate was staring into the face of madness and she knew it. "Jim Chopin knows everything I know," she said. "He'll figure it out, sooner or later."

Christie laughed. "What he knows and what he can prove are two different things."

"They'll trace the rifle through the bullets."

"They'll have to find the bullet first. They'll have to find the rifle first. They'll have to find your body first, and I've got plans for that." She laughed again. "I've always got a plan, Kate."

Dan, Kate thought, talk about Dan. "You went after Dan because he was the chief ranger, and he could help you get easements so you can develop the land. The land you think you're going to inherit from your mother."

"And now my father," Christie said. "At first, all I wanted to do was kill them. I picked Riley up in Montana, and I saw right away how I could put him to work for me.

"Then I got here, and I saw how well-off both my loving parents were, and I thought, Why not me?" Her gaze turned inward, and Kate edged a little farther around the stove. "Why shouldn't all that lovely money come to me?" Her face contorted. "They owed me!"

Kate remembered Christie cozying up to Pete Heiman at the potlatch. "You're about to dump Dan, aren't you? For Pete Heiman."

Christie grimaced. "He wasn't supposed to get himself fired."

"And Pete has so much more power."

"There is that," the other woman admitted. "We helpless types do like a strong man to lean on."

"What if John hadn't killed himself?"

"He would have." Christie smiled again, and Kate repressed a shiver. "He had no idea who I was the first time I went to the lodge. I didn't tell him until after I'd been there twice."

Kate felt ill. "You didn't."

Christie laughed. "Of course I did. Like I said, I've had a lot of experience playing daddy. Be a shame not to put it to good use." She shrugged, managing to make it look graceful even from the inside of a parka. She'd kept her gloves on, too. Cold air was pouring in through the open door.

Kate tried not to shiver. "Whose rifle is that?"

"Whose do you think?"

Kate thought of the second empty cradle in John Letourneau's gun cabinet. No one would ever miss it.

Christie shook her hair out of her eyes, her face bright with triumph. "So, maybe six months, maybe a year from now, I'll 'discover' my parentage. Something drew me here to the Park, something irresistible, calling me. I didn't know what it was, but I just couldn't fight it. And look what I found—my one true love and my birth parents, at one blow! What a story, how romantic. They'll probably make a movie of the week out of it. I'll be happy to sell the rights to it, for a fair price."

Kate wondered why murderers were so in love with the sound of their own voices. Still, the longer Christie talked, the longer Kate had to figure out a plan. Any minute now, she would. She edged another inch across the floor. If she pounced, she could grab the barrel of the rifle; if she was lucky, maybe even before Christie could get off a shot. Or she could dive behind the couch. And do what? Throw books?

"Pete and I will marry, of course," Christie said dreamily. "He'll like the idea of a landed wife. And then we'll see what we can do about breaking that land trust and putting the land to more profitable use. Pete thinks the road into the Park should be paved, or so he was telling me this afternoon. We might even subdivide." Christie smiled. "Just this one little problem, then I'll be on my way."

Her eyes went flat. The barrel straightened, the muzzle zeroed in on Kate's chest, and her finger began to squeeze the trigger. Kate took a flying leap over the back of the couch, but not soon enough. Christie swung the rifle, following her. The shot thundered in the little room and filled it with the acrid smell of gun smoke. The bullet hit Kate in the side and lifted her up and back, slamming her into the bookcase. She fell behind the couch, caught beneath an avalanche of books.

"Damn it," she said, irritated. Looking down, she saw blood rapidly soaking the front of her shirt. It felt warm and wet. It was a new shirt, too, and Pendletons didn't come cheap. "Damn it," she said again, more mildly this time.

Christie's face appeared over the back of the couch, flushed, radiant, triumphant. As she raised the rifle a second time, Mutt juggernauted through the open door like an avenging angel and hit Christie in the small of the back, knocking her into the woodstove. There was a sizzle of burning skin and a cry.

Christie got off one more shot before the rifle spun out

of her hands and landed beneath the table. She reached for it, but Mutt's teeth sank in long before her arm got there, and the last thing Kate heard before the spreading pain pulled her under was Christie's scream.

12

When Kate woke, it was to pain, the whole left side of her body infused with it. She muttered an inarticulate protest. She hated pain. Pain hurt. She tried to say so.

"It's all right," a voice said; "we'll give you something. Drink this."

She drank, felt the prick of a needle, slid back down into darkness.

She dreamed in bits and pieces. An anxious whining, a sandpapery tongue. Jim swearing. Hands hurting her, something tight around her chest. Hands on her shoulders. Hands on her feet. The jolting agony of a drive in the back of someone's truck. A strong arm holding her steady, a solid shoulder against her cheek. The drone of an airplane engine, with her flat on her back on the floor, her legs beneath the pilot's seat, her eyes staring up at the bare ribs of the fuselage.

Waking the second time, she found a woman staring down at her. "Hello, Kate," she said. "I'm Adrienne Giroux. I'm your doctor."

"Where—"

"At the hospital in Ahtna."

Kate tried to raise her head. "What happened to me?"

"You were shot," Giroux said without inflection. Her hand was steady on Kate's wrist. She had brown hair pulled back in a twist, a softly rounded figure beneath a starchy white coat.

Kate closed her eyes. "I remember now," she said after a moment. She opened her eyes. "What happened to the woman who shot me?"

"She's here, too, just down the hall. Under guard, so don't worry." Giroux hesitated. "She's in a lot worse shape than you are. We might wind up having to take off her arm."

"Good," Kate said, and slid downward to darkness again.

When she woke up the third time, she was alone in the room. There was the muted clink of glassware and cutlery in the hall, and a moment later the door swung open. "Miss Shugak?" A round red face peered in. "Oh good, you're awake."

She was served lunch—a soggy ham sandwich, a tasteless macaroni salad, and a banana. She forced it all down because she knew the sooner she regained her strength, the sooner she could go home and cook for herself.

None of the meals that followed over the next day and a half were any better. She didn't have anything to read and there was nothing to watch on the television suspended from the ceiling over the foot of her bed. She was so bored, she could have screamed, and she was a little hurt that she hadn't had any visitors. Ruthe had had visitors non-stop.

Before dinner the next day, the door opened. Kate looked toward it and all she saw was a gray streak cannoning toward her. "Mutt!" she said, and was ashamed that her voice trembled. "Where did you come from?"

"I thought you could use some company," said a voice

from the door. "I brought you some books, too." Jim Chopin set a sack on the table next to the bed.

Mutt had leapt to the bed and was nosing Kate all over, an anxious whine coming from her throat. "I'm all right, girl," Kate said, half laughing, half crying. She winced when a leg bumped into her side, but it was the best pain she'd ever felt and she wouldn't have traded it for no pain and no Mutt.

"She has to behave," Jim said. "I had to get a special dispensation from the doctor to get her in here."

"She'll behave," Kate said, knotting her hands in Mutt's ruff and shaking her. "Won't you, girl?" She looked up at Jim.

He wouldn't meet her eyes. "Ethan told me to tell you that Johnny's fine. Johnny told me to tell you that Gal's fine. Giroux said I couldn't stay long, so I'll—" He jerked a head at the door and retreated a step.

"You brought Mutt to me?" To her horror, her voice began to quaver.

He shrugged. "Yeah. Well. I better go. I've got—"

By a sheer effort of will, she mastered her voice. "Jim."

He fell silent.

"Thank you," she whispered.

"You're welcome. I mean, it's nothing. I just, I—Jesus, Kate, I thought you were dead."

His face was pale and strained. "Mutt came for me; she practically took the door of the cabin off. She bullied me into my clothes and into Billy's Explorer and down the road. It was all her." He paused, thinking of the last time he and Mutt had ridden to Kate's rescue, not near long enough ago, when Kate had been dumped like so much garbage in a landfill outside Ahtna. He didn't know how many more times his heart was going to stand up to that.

"I thought you were dead," he repeated. "There was so much blood—all over you, all over the floor." He stopped again, then swallowed with difficulty. All over the floor where they had lain together just days before. "At first, I couldn't find a pulse." Mostly because he'd been so scared, but he wasn't going to say that. Not yet anyway. "I wrapped you up as best I could." He shook his head and gave a brief unhumorous laugh. "I couldn't find hardly anything to use for bandages—I'd used up pretty much everything they had on Ruthe. In the end, I tore my shirt into strips and used that."

Mutt lay down next to Kate. She watched him over the big gray head.

He took a deep breath. "Longest drive of my life, longest flight. It was blowing snow and fog by then, I took off and landed both below minimums. I'm probably going to hear about that from the FAA."

He didn't sound overly concerned about it. She watched him twist the ball cap with the trooper emblem on the front between his hands. "I thought you were dead," he said, his voice so low that she could barely hear it. "I thought I'd lost you."

It was very quiet in the room for a few moments. Kate opened her mouth and found that she had to clear her throat before she could speak. "What about Christie?"

"She's down the hall."

"They told me."

"Under guard, in case she gets up, which they tell me she won't anytime soon. Mutt—" Mutt's ears went up at this mention of her name by her idol, who stepped near enough to reach her ears and give her a good scratch. "She's alive, but I think Mutt was kind of in a hurry. Plus maybe a little pissed off." Mutt's tail thumped gently on the bed. "Christie's probably going to lose that arm." He shrugged. "But then she won't need it where she's going."

His hand slipped from Mutt's ears to cup Kate's cheek. "I thought you were dead."

He was leaning forward when they heard the squeak of

wheels in the corridor, the jingle of dishes, followed by a knock on the door. "Oh, yummy," Kate said. "Dinner."

He didn't know whether to curse or laugh. Instead, he looked down at her and smiled. "You want me to bring you a burger?"

She looked at him with her heart in her eyes.

"Poor John," Ruthe said.

Her skin was almost translucent, but she was conscious, and there was a faint flush of color along her exquisite cheekbones. Every doctor and nurse in the place was head over heels in love with her, naturally, and Kate's visit had been constantly interrupted by this one or that wanting to take Ruthe's temperature or blood pressure, or plump up her pillows, or tempt her taste buds with some god-awful dish from the hospital cafeteria. A surgeon who wasn't even attending her case scored heavily when he brought in a box of fried chicken and french fries. The smell of deep-fried chicken almost obscured the Phisohex-like smell endemic to all hospitals, making Kate's mouth water. Ruthe's graceful thanks brought a flush to the surgeon's cheek and a gleam to his eye, and he floated out the door with a smile on his face.

Not bad, Kate thought, and wondered if she would be able to pull that off at seventy plus.

"Here," Ruthe said, passing her the box. "I can't, not yet."

Kate, wrapped like a mummy and tucked into a wheelchair, didn't even try to talk her out of it. It took real nobility to offer to share with Jim. He accepted with alacrity, and she tried not to call him names inside her own head. Mutt gave her a pitiful look. "Chicken bones are bad for you," she told the wolf, and tucked into a drumstick.

"Poor John," Ruthe said again. "He really loved Dina." She turned her eyes from the window to where the two of them sat side by side, eating. "How's the chicken?"

"Sure you won't try a piece?" Kate said.

"Certain sure," Ruthe said. "Besides, I'm afraid to get in the middle of you two. Might tear my hand off."

Jim, drumstick raised, laughed. Kate, mouth full of thigh, didn't.

Ruthe had woken from her coma two days after Kate had been brought in. Much to the trooper's frustration, she still couldn't remember anything from the day of her attack, even though the doctors had said that was to be expected. "Short-term memory is what goes first after a violent attack," they'd said, and Jim snapped, snarled, and growled, but in the end, because he'd had experience with a head injury and a subsequent short-term memory loss himself the summer before, he subsided into a frustrated silence. "Don't harass her," they had warned him. "She doesn't need to do anything right now but get well. Don't mess with that."

So this was strictly a social call, except that Ruthe wanted to know everything that had happened since she'd been away, including why Kate was one door down.

She was paler when they finished. Kate told her about the potlatch, and the picture, the original of which she had had Jim bring to the hospital.

Ruthe wept at the sight of it. "I remember that day," she said, mopping her eyes with the Kleenex Kate moved within reach. "Mudhole was starting air tours from Cordova to the mine. That was the inaugural flight. He loaded up everyone he could think of and gave us the VIP treatment—had champagne and caviar waiting for us when we got there. We all got a little tight."

"Emaa had champagne?" Kate said, awed.

"We all did." Ruthe's smile faded. "That was the day it started, I think. Dina sat next to John. They hit it off. I think it was more chemistry than it was anything else, but it was strong and it was immediate, and a month later, they were married."

Kate didn't look at her, not wanting to exacerbate Ruthe's pain. "That must have hurt."

"What? Why?"

Kate looked up. "Well, I—" She cast about wildly for some way to say it without sticking the knife in. "Dina left you. You know, for John."

"Oh," Ruthe said, starting to smile, then began to laugh. "Oh. Right. I forgot." She started to cough.

"Are you okay?" Jim said, standing up in alarm, box in one hand, french fry in the other. "Should we call somebody?"

She waved them off with a weak hand. "I'm all right. I can't laugh yet, either."

"What's so funny?" Kate said, bewildered.

Ruthe mopped her eyes and smiled at Kate. "Dina didn't leave me. Not in the way you mean."

"What?" Kate said. "I'm sorry, I don't—"

"Dina and I were never a couple."

Kate gaped at her. After a moment, she recovered and said, "But you—I thought—we all thought that—"

"We knew what you all thought," Ruthe said, grinning. "We used to laugh about it. Hell, back then, everybody thought all WASPs were bull dykes. Stood to reason. Real women didn't want to learn to fly." She made a face. "You should have seen Mac Devlin's expression the first time he met us. You would have thought we had horns and tails. When we were younger, it was kind of fun. Wasn't a bad come-on, either. You'd be amazed at the number of men who are absolutely convinced that all one of *those* women needs is the love of a good man to turn her around." She grinned again. "We let the likelier ones try to convince us." She added, "Of course, there were always a few who were praying for a threesome. We never went for that. Well, hardly ever."

"Okay," Kate said, "too much information."

"I'm kidding!" Ruthe said, and started to laugh again. "God, if you could see the expression on *your* face!"

Kate could feel her neck going red, and she could hear Jim starting to laugh, too. "Did Emaa know?"

"Of course she knew; she used to chase around with us. That girl could party us all right into the ground."

"Stop," Kate said desperately, "please, I'm begging you, stop right there."

"She was a looker when she was old," Jim said, "I bet she could knock your eyes out when she was younger."

"Do. Not. Go. There," Kate said.

Jim met Ruthe's eyes for a pregnant moment. Sometimes it was just too easy.

"What about their daughter?" Kate said. It was the only way she could get out of the hole she was in, and then Jim gave her a dagger look and she remembered they weren't supposed to try to jog Ruthe's memory. But Ruthe gave a last chuckle, coughed into a Kleenex, and said, "What daughter?"

There was a brief silence. "Christie Turner," Kate said.

Ruthe's brow puckered. "Christie Turner? Oh, you mean Bernie's new barmaid. What about her?"

"She's John and Dina's daughter, Ruthe."

Ruthe stared at Kate. "I beg your pardon?"

"Christie Turner is John and Dina's daughter."

Another silence. "Are you sure?" Ruthe said at last.

"We've seen the birth certificate. She was born in Seattle, ten months to the day after the date on the marriage certificate. Father, John Letourneau. Mother, Dina Willner."

"Oh," Ruthe said. She closed her eyes against sudden remembered pain. "Oh," she said again, a drawn-out expression of realization. "So that was it."

"What was it?"

"About two months after their marriage broke up, Dina came up with this idea to do a marketing tour of the camp

Outside. I figured she wanted to get away for a while, so I helped her set it up. Eco-tourism was just starting to catch on, and I thought it was a good idea to put us out in front on it. I offered to go with her, but she wanted to go alone. She left after we shut down the camp for the winter. Right around the first of October, I think it was." She was silent for a moment. "She wrote after three months, saying she was going to a WASP reunion in Texas. After that, she was going to visit her mother, then friends. And after that, one of her teachers. After a while, I stopped expecting her home. And then, there she was, walking in the door."

"She never told you?"

"No." Ruthe closed her eyes and shook her head. "Oh, Dina. She didn't have to do it all alone. She should have known I would have stood by her. Helped. She could have brought the baby home. We could have raised her."

Would it have made any difference? Kate wondered, remembering the pride and triumph in Christie's crazy eyes just before she pulled the trigger. "She put the baby up for adoption," Kate said.

"And that baby was Christie Turner?"

"Yes."

"I want to see her."

Kate looked at Jim. "That's not possible, Ruthe."

So then, of course, they had to fill in all the discreet blanks they had left out.

"Her childhood was like something out of Dickens," Jim said somberly. "There's a cop who owes me at SPD; he managed to pull her juvie file." He shook his head. "There's always someone who slips through the cracks, and twenty-five years ago that someone was Christie Turner. The couple who adopted her also took in foster children. There were never fewer than a dozen kids in the house. Apparently, the father took his pick of the girls. Christie was a beautiful child—the cop sent a picture—and she was her father's special girl from the time she was four."

Kate instantly felt the sick rage she always felt when con-
fronted with child abuse. She wanted to rescue the child,
even if that child was Christie Turner. She wanted to geld
the abuser. She wanted to make it stop, all of it, just stop.

Jim saw the look on her face, and he turned to Ruthe.
"Can you handle this? Most of it's pretty hard to take. We
don't have to talk about it now."

"Yes, we do," Ruthe said. "When it's cold, you have to
dive in; you can't stand around shilly-shallying on the shore.
And this kind of story never gets any better in the telling
anyway."

"All right. When the guy finally got caught, the whole
story came out, and you're right, it wasn't pretty. One of
the other children testified at the trial. Apparently, they
rented the kids out for just about anything you could imagine—prostitution and drug running, just for starters, running scams when they got older. They shoplifted most of
their food and clothing. The only time they went to school
was when the school sent the cops to the house to find out
why they weren't in class."

He set the box of chicken, the bones gnawed clean, on
the floor. Mutt sidled over, sniffed, and nosed the box to a
corner of the room, out of Kate's sight. "I called the girl
who testified when they finally got caught, and the case
wound up actually being prosecuted. She's twenty-one now,
in college, looks like she's going to be all right. She said
Christie was always talking about her birth parents and how
she'd been stolen away from them, and how they were coming back for her." He shook his head. "Classic orphan fan-
tasy."

Ruthe winced. "She wasn't an orphan."

"She ran away for the last time at sixteen. Her juvie record ends there."

"How did she find out who her parents were, and where
they lived?"

"I traced Dina's obstetrician to Seattle," Jim said. "He's

dead, but his son took over his practice, and the nurse who attended the birth is still alive. She said they hired a young blond woman about six years ago as a receptionist. She stayed for about ten days, and when she left, some files were missing. Dina's file was among them." He paused. "I'm guessing she stole the other files to cover the theft of the one file that mattered. Christie learned early how to cover her tracks."

"How did she find the doctor?"

"Adopted children can apply to find out who their birth parents are nowadays."

"I know, but I thought there were safeguards, that there had to be consent on both sides before any information could be revealed."

"This girl learned how to work the system at a very early age," Jim said. "I doubt that a bureaucracy as byzantine as Social Services stood a chance."

"She contacted John first," Kate said after a moment. "She told me."

Jim nodded. "Would have been a hell of a scene."

Kate tried not to think about just what kind of scene it had been.

"John would have hated that," Ruthe said.

"And that's how he knew who she was," Kate said, "and why he knew who had killed Dina."

"And he made a false confession and killed himself to deflect suspicion?" Jim said, still skeptical. "Why bother? I never would have been able to prove anything."

"Guilt," Kate said. "Seventeen different kinds of guilt." Especially after Christie had seduced him, with the full knowledge of who he was. She still couldn't think of it without feeling sick.

"Dina was dead," Ruthe said.

They looked at her.

"He really loved her," Ruthe told them. "John really loved Dina. She left him, he didn't leave her."

"Why did she leave him?"

"She never said."

Kate thought again of the tiny, crowded cabin and the enormous, empty lodge. She knew why Dina had left John.

"He was too proud to fight the divorce, and he was angry at her for making him look ridiculous, but there was never anyone else for John but Dina. And then she was dead." Ruthe shifted, and Kate brought the blanket up around her shoulders. "And here was the only thing left to him of her, a daughter he hadn't even known existed, a daughter who told him she hated him, a daughter who might have just confessed to matricide. Maybe he thought he could save her. Maybe he couldn't do anything but try."

There was little of the martyr about John Letourneau, Kate thought. But she understood a little about guilt.

Families. Mothers, fathers, children. There was no explaining them, and there was no understanding the wonderful and terrible things they did to and for one another. She thought of her mother, passed out in the snow, dead of hypothermia before her daughter was four. And Stephan, Kate's father, following so soon afterward. If Stephan had loved Zoya so much that he could not bear to live life without her, even if he had to leave his daughter behind, why couldn't John love Dina enough to die for the sake of their only child? Maybe it didn't matter that John hadn't known of her existence until that fall, when she had shown up on his doorstep and pushed herself into his life.

Kate thought of Johnny, who had pushed himself into her life.

"Poor John," Ruthe said sadly, breaking into Kate's thoughts. "And poor Christie. Poor lonely little girl."

Kate thought of Dina, dead, and Ruthe, nearly so. Not to mention herself. Her hand fell to Mutt's head and tightened in the thick gray ruff. Christie could have killed Mutt, too. She would have if Mutt hadn't been smarter and faster and stronger. She gave the ruff a shake and Mutt sat up and leaned against her chair. "What about that other girl, the one who testified at the trial of Christie's adoptive parents?"

"What about her?"

"She went through the same things Christie went through, and she didn't have to kill anyone to get to where she is now. I mean, damn it. At some point, I don't care what kind of life you've had, how awful your parents were to you or how mean your teachers or how nasty your class-mates, at some point you have to step up and take respon-sibility for your own actions and your own life. Okay, I admit, Christie Turner had it rough, few rougher. That doesn't mean she gets a free ride. Not from me anyway."

There was a brief silence.

Ruthe looked at Jim. "Does she have a lawyer?"

"I don't think so," Jim said.

"Get her one," Ruthe said. "I'll pay."

"Ruthe—"

"A good one, Kate."

"Ruthe—"

"Right away, Kate," Ruthe said sternly. "Before the storm troopers"—Jim made an inarticulate sound of protest at this—"beat a confession out of her."

"All right, Ruthe," Kate said, bowing her head. "I will." She looked at Jim. "What about Riley Higgins?"

"He's out of jail. He's got a job sweeping out the Kin-nikinick Bar, but I don't know how long he'll last."

Kate wondered who had gotten Riley Higgins his job.

"He can come back to the camp if he wants to," Ruthe said.

"I'll tell him," Jim said.

Ruthe wanted to return to the cabin as soon as possible.

"Maybe you should think about finding somewhere closer to town," Jim suggested.

"Like where?" Ruthe smiled. "Camp Teddy is my home. I want to get back to it as soon as possible."

As Jim was wheeling Kate out the door, Mutt padding

along behind them, Ruthe said, "Kate? Do me a favor? Find out who's John's heir, and if they'd like to sell the lodge."

"Are you serious?"

"Never more so," Ruthe said, with a fair assumption of her usual good cheer. She actually winked. "Someone's going to get hold of that prime piece of riverfront property. It might as well be the Kanuyaq Land Trust."

13

Jim brought the Cessna from Tok and flew Kate home to Niniltna two days later. Bobby, Dinah, and Katya and Auntie Vi were there to greet her on the airstrip. Auntie Vi wanted her to come stay while she recuperated, but Kate refused. She was like Ruthe. She wanted to go home.

So Bobby tucked her into his truck and ferried her twenty-five miles down the road, and Dinah and Jim, who had followed in Billy's Explorer, walked her down the path to the homestead, Mutt trotting anxious circles around them as they went. "Johnny's at Ethan's; he's got Gal with him. He's going to leave you alone for a couple of days," Dinah said as if by rote. "Ethan says he'll be over this evening."

"No," Kate said. "Dinah, could you stop in and ask him not to? I just want to see if I can get up the ladder and sleep in my own bed. Tell him I'll be over tomorrow."

"Okay." Dinah exchanged a glance with Bobby. They both looked at Jim, who remained impassive.

They settled her in, fussing over the woodstove, overfilling the kettle, and bringing her comforter down from the loft. "I'm okay, guys," she said when she could stand it no longer. "Go."

"Okay," Dinah repeated. "I'll be back out tomorrow." She saw the look on Kate's face and said, "If I don't come and report back to Auntie Vi, she'll be here, and she'll bring all the other aunties with her."

It was only too true. "All right. See you tomorrow, then."

Jim waited until Dinah was out the door. "By the way, Kate."

"What now?" she said grouchily.

He grinned at her, the wide white grin that made her want to reach for her rifle. "I wanted you to be the first to know," he said, settling the ball cap over his ears. His uniform jacket was neat and clean, the lighter blue uniform slacks with the gold stripe down the sides creased to a knife edge, his boots freshly polished. He looked every inch the trooper today, immaculate, authoritative, totally in charge.

"Know what?" Kate said, dragging her eyes to his face with difficulty.

The grin widened. She measured the distance between the couch and the gun rack over the door. "I'm moving my post," he said.

"Moving your post? You mean you're being transferred?" She tried to tell herself that she was feeling relief, not dismay.

"No, moving my post from Tok."

"Moving it?" With sudden foreboding, she said, "Where?"

"To Niniltna."

She gaped at him.

His dimples deepened. How had she never noticed those dimples before? "Yeah. I'll be around all the time now." He stepped to the door and tipped his hat.

"Be seeing you, Kate." The grin flashed. "A lot of you."

14

Two days later, Dan came to the homestead. "I'm sorry, Kate," he said.

"Get your ass in here and close the door," Kate said. "You're letting the cold in."

"I didn't know if I'd be welcome or not."

"You want to drink your coffee or wear it?"

His face cleared.

"What did you think you knew?" she said as they ate homemade bread, her first batch since she'd gotten out of the hospital, spread with butter and strawberry preserves.

He sighed and put his bread down, half-eaten. "She asked a lot of questions about Ruthe and Dina."

"So did everybody. They weren't exactly low-profile."

"Don't try to make me feel better about this, Kate," he said, looking sober. "Christie asked a lot of questions, and when Dina died, I should have told you or Jim. She wanted to know about the restrictions on developing privately owned property within Park boundaries, for god's sake. Why would she care, unless she owned some? She didn't, not then. I should have noticed. I should have figured she was only using me to help her get what she wanted. Damn it, Kate, I just feel so damn stupid."

"You were in love," she said.

"No, I was in heat," he said. "You can lead even the smartest man most anywhere by his cock."

She tried not to wince.

"Sorry," he said. "Hey, did you hear about Jim Chopin moving his post to Niniltna?"

"Yes," she said.

"Sure will make life easier for me," he said. "Long as I've got my job anyway."

"They haven't fired you yet, I take it?"

"No. They even revoked my suspension. I think Pete might have had something to do with that."

"Why?"

"He stopped by the Step, told me not to worry." Dan's grin was a pale shadow of its former self, but it was out where you could see it. "Told me I owed him."

"He would."

"Well, I do. And I won't mind paying off when the time comes." He finished his bread and coffee. "You going to be okay?"

"I'm going to be okay," she said.

She watched him leave from the doorway. Snow was falling, coating the semicircle of buildings in the little clearing with a fresh layer, filling in the old blemishes, covering up the new. A new snowfall was a great place from which to start over.

The next day, she walked up to the steps of the Int-Hout homestead and knocked on the door.

She had rehearsed what she was going to say all the previous night, that morning, and all the way to Ethan's. Not the truth, of course, never the truth, not if she could help it, not even when she figured out what it was herself.

Ethan, she was going to say, I'm just not ready, and I don't know if I'll ever be. What we've been working on is the residue of a high school crush. If we'd ever managed to make it to bed together in college, we wouldn't be sniffing around each other now. I'm moving on. You need to, too.

Short, to the point, and the absolute truth, and only she needed to know it wasn't all the truth. She knocked again. Footsteps came toward the door. She squared her shoulders and prepared to lower the boom.

The door opened. A large woman with freckled skin and wild red hair stood in the opening.

"Hello, Margaret," Kate said.

"Hi, Kate. I want my husband back."

Over Margaret's shoulder, she saw Ethan with his lap full of twins. He looked over their heads at Kate, his face full of shamefaced apology.

"He's all yours," Kate said, and with those words, a huge weight fell from her shoulders.

"Good. You can have this back, too." Margaret reached behind her and pulled Johnny forward. Johnny was dressed in a parka and down pants and was carrying a duffel bag. Gal's indignant face poked out of the front of his parka and she yowled at Kate and hissed at Mutt. Margaret must have started assembling the package when she first heard Kate's snow machine coming.

"I'll take him," Kate said.

Margaret closed the door in their faces.

"Why are you smiling?" Johnny said.

"Was I?" Kate said, and started to laugh. She stood on the porch, shoulders shaking, trying not to laugh too hard, hand pressed to her side, which she was still afraid was going to fall off if she moved the wrong way. "Sorry," she said, the last chuckle draining away. She put her hands on Johnny's shoulders and looked down into his face. Not so far down, and not for long. "I owe you an apology, Johnny."

"What? What for?"

"I should have let you stay at the homestead from the beginning, instead of farming you out to Ethan. I'm your home now."

"Oh." He was confused but willing. "Okay. I guess." He was further confused when she pulled him in for a bear hug, and the hell with the damage to her side. He trailed her bemusedly to the snow machine. "So . . . does this mean that you're not going to . . . uh . . . you and Ethan aren't . . ."

"No. We're not."

"Good."

"Yeah?" She pulled his hat down over his eyes.

"Yeah." He shoved it back up. "I like Ethan and all, but he's kind of, well, static, you know? Sort of running in the same gear all the time. That could get old."

"It could," Kate admitted.

He loaded the duffel on the trailer. Gal meowed imperiously from his parka and he petted her absently. "Dad liked Chopper Jim."

Kate paused in the act of starting the snow machine. "What?" Where had that come from?

"Yeah. He said"—Johnny scratched beneath his cap—"he said he was the best trooper he knew and a good man, even if he was a colossal pain in the ass."

Kate relaxed. "Yeah, that sounds like he liked him a whole hell of a lot."

Johnny grinned. "He said the same thing about you."

It surprised a laugh out of her. "Mount up, mouthie."

"What are we going to do now?"

"We're going to build an extension to my cabin," Kate said, grinning at him. "A room for you. How are you with tools?"

He looked at her, uncertain. "What about my mom? She knows where you live. She could find me."

"She could," Kate agreed.

"She could make me go with her."

"Could she?"

She watched him think it over, and she was still watching when his face split in a sudden grin. "No. No, I don't think she could."

The grin made him so like his father that her breath caught in her throat. "I don't, either." She started the snow machine. "Get on."

It was crowded on the seat between Kate, Johnny, Gal, and Mutt, but they were all going home together.